HOT OFF THE PRESS

A CHARITY ANTHOLOGY

DISCLAIMER: "This is a work of fiction. Names, characters, places and incidents are products of the author's imagination and are used fictitiously. Any resemblance to actual events, locales or persons, living or dead, is entirely coincidental."

Copyright © 2022 Red Cape Publishing

All rights reserved.

Cover Art by David Paul Harris

www.davidpaulharris.com

Contents

Foreword by Jay Michaels	5
Introduction by MJ Dixon	7
Fight or Flight by David Owain Hughes	9
Amorousness of the Necrotic Divinity by Michael 'The Dedman' Jones	10
Great White-Water Rafting by Madeline Deering	11
House Call by Martin W. Payne	13
A Return to Light by Cortney Palm	17
The Hair by Tracy Allen	21
Splitting Headache by Jaysen P. Buterin	24
No Matter What by Joe Graciano	28
A Piece of You by Nat Whiston	31
The Rise of the Scarecrows by Callum Pearce	35
The Promise by Kenn Hoekstra	39
The Executioners by Dineta Williams-Trigg	41
Thoughts on Visiting the Man with the Hood by Rollin Jewett	43
It's What's Inside that Counts by Lyndsey Ellis-Holloway	46
Beastiary by MJ Dixon	50
Casey by James Jobling	51
Lake Woodboard by Reyna Young	54
Night Drive by Melanie Vukusich	58
Meth Gator: The Dealer by John Shatzer	62
Ouija Printer by Killian H. Gore	66
Sweet Revenge by Tori Danielle Romero	70
Mr Taylor by Sarah Schultz	74
My Summer Job by Singh Lall & Maya Lall	77
Blue Light of Death by Justin Terrell	78
Do the Devil's Work by Dean Kilbey	82
The Tapes by Danni Winn	88

Open Doorways by Peter F Mahoney	92
Knickers by Tony Sands	96
The Room at the End by Patrick Krause	99
Blue Moon Bottling by Monster Smith	103
A Better Place by Hal C.F. Astell	107
Misphonia by Alain Elliott	111
The Mysterious Case of the Patch of Damp by Tony Mardon	113
Being Normal by Astrid Addams	115
Mirror Mirror by Chris McAuley	119
The Wolf in the Darkness by Craig David Dowsett	122
The Rise of the Sanguinista by Cortney Palm	124
A Long Way Down by Bill Oberst Jr.	128
Inside Voice A.K.A. Research by Adam Marcus	129
The Circle Inside the Triangle by Jonathan Patrick Hughes	132
The Present by Philip Rogers	137
Unsolved: True Crime Hits Home by Debbie Rochon	139
The Checklist by Matt Doyle	143
Other Titles	147

Hot Off the Press

Foreword

Here is a collection of tales of terror from some of the world's most prominent author, playwrights, and screenwriters. A rare and valuable treat for lovers of the genre or for anyone who likes a good fright.

My sincerest thanks to all the authors who contributed their great talent to this book. But this collection pulls double duty. Maybe it's about monsters but they are also battling a monster as well - Angelman Syndrome.

Angelman Syndrome is a complex genetic disorder that primarily affects the nervous system. While it is not known to cut life short, the souls afflicted with this disorder will suffer delayed development, intellectual disability, severe speech impairment, and problems with movement and balance. They will need support throughout their entire lives. My heart goes out to them and to their families who are there for them and who must prepare for when they are not.

Angelman Syndrome is clever. It misleads you to think it is a form of autism due to similar symptoms, including hyperactive behavior, speech problems and specific recognizable movement, but a child with Angelman Syndrome is highly sociable, unlike a child with autism. A child with Angelman Syndrome still wants to belong.

A piece of the Dracula lore, oft forgotten in film versions, purports that the vampire must be welcomed into a home, or they cannot enter. The Frankenstein Monster, as depicted by Boris Karloff, is someone who feels he just doesn't belong. Even the cinematic Wolfman is someone who stands alone amid his afflictions.

Any lover of the genre, when describing their youth, invariably says they were the "weird kid" ... the outsider ... alone. Who better than those of us who treasure the macabre genre to understand the deep emotional element

A Charity Anthology

that comes with affliction. The feeling of being alone and even forgotten.

For children with Angelman Syndrome and their families, life can be a real horror story. The fear of being abandoned is a very real tale of terror.

Proceeds from this book will go to support FAST UK, the Foundation for Angelman Syndrome Therapeutics, whose mission for nearly 15 years, has been to **cure Angelman Syndrome**. With operations in Australia, Canada, France, Italy, Spain and the UK, FAST has become the largest non-governmental funder of Angelman Syndrome research. FAST brings together a multidisciplinary team of more than two-dozen scientists from top research universities and pharmaceutical companies to battle this monster.

We, who populate the pages of this book, are not doctors. But we understand the sense of loneliness that an affliction of this caliber can bring to a family, so we want to help.

My deepest gratitude to Donovan Smith and Red Cape Publishing for allowing me – and all my colleagues in this exciting book – to get involved. And a truly heartfelt thanks to all of you – the readers. Thank you for your purchase, allowing organizations like FAST to help battle the darkness of this syndrome and to bring those afflicted closer to the daylight of success.

Jay Michaels
Professor of Communications and Media Culture
Horror Film Historian

Introduction

I've written horror stories my whole life, putting people in the most horrific situations imaginable. It always seemed like fantasy in a lot of ways. However, in August 2020, when we discovered that our son had Angelman Syndrome, I suddenly felt a completely different kind of horror, one that had robbed my son of the chance of having a 'normal' life and all the things we had taken for granted. The things that he would 'just do', such as talk, walk, play sports, enjoy the movies, go to high school, to college, get married, have his own children… they were all wiped out in the blink of an eye. It was worse than any horror I've ever placed a fictional character in. I wouldn't have wished it upon any of them, even in fantasy.

We love our son. He's the best. Despite his condition, he is amazingly loving, incredibly tenacious and spectacularly resilient. He achieves amazing things every day, and he speaks in his own way, his own personal language. He moves around in ways (and at speeds) you wouldn't expect from a child who hasn't taken his first steps. He's amazing and he often makes the 'horror' of that diagnosis seem distant in a way.

My wife often says, "He's never met a stranger," and it's true, he bewitches everyone he meets with his wonderful, cheerful, personality. I'd almost like to say, I wouldn't change a thing. But that's not exactly true…

…because I would cure him in a second if I could.

F.A.S.T are doing some amazing work in the pursuit of curing Angelman Syndrome and the

A Charity Anthology

research they help fund could lead to our son, one day, leading a much more normal life that he is currently able. It's why I'm incredibly grateful to Donovan and Red Cape Publishing for choosing F.A.S.T as the charity for the proceeds of this book.

Thanks for reading.

MJ

Fight or Flight

David Owain Hughes

He kicked open the doors to the disused cinema, fixed his crooked dog's collar, and cocked his modified crossbow capable of firing fifty stakes.

"Come get some, you blood-sucking hell beasts!" he said. "I'm here to kick arse for my Lord!"

Vampire bats swooped, avoiding shafts of daylight coming in through the doors, as he opened fire.

"*Aarggh*!" he screamed, his bolts spearing the creatures. "I'll return you to Lucifer!"

When his crossbow ran dry, he tossed holy water hand grenades, but their number were too great, and they fell on him, wrapping him in a black, screeching blanket of hades…

A Charity Anthology

Amorousness of the Necrotic Divinity

Michael 'The Dedman' Jones

In my nightmares She is there as we walk hand
in hand through the graveyard's foggy shroud,
An icy cold grip binds me alongside the Goddess
as my emotions are fearful and yet proud?

Cold, unflinching eyes of milky white bore into
mine with the promise of ethereal pleasure,
Long red hair still flows with the smell of dirt
and fetid flowers, such an olfactory treasure!

The moon highlights skin of alabaster and gray,
yet no trace of maggot or rot to be seen,
Her body exquisitely accented by a flawless
burial gown of silk and lace fit for only a queen.

Romanticism be damned as wings as black as
midnight unfurl the lust that exists between us,
Lips blood red part as She leans in for Death's
kiss, an onyx tongue searching in a matter so
treasonous.

Thoughts of unsanctified copulation inundate my
thoughts as Her embrace tightens and claws extend,
There is no resistance or want to escape the
insatiable lust that we together shall transcend.

The frostiness of Her flesh belies the heat of
passion that wells from the Goddess' carnal scheme,
And as I pass through the gates of Damnation for
my sins I simply wish harder for this eternal
dream...

Hot Off the Press

Great White-Water Rafting

Madeline Deering

Jimmy and his friends drove down an abandoned dirt road looking for the perfect spot. It was their last day before graduation, when these four best friends may never see each other again. Jimmy was the alpha male, Olivia was his preppy girlfriend, Donny was the nice guy, kind of a nerd, (he knew how to solve equations and shit). Jenny was the nice girl. The four were attention seekers looking for the next big rush. And then they passed it: the perfect spot.

Jimmy stopped the car and grabbed his rafting gear, as did everyone else. A raft, life vests, and of course the most important thing: beer.

From a distance it just looked like trees, but beneath the trees was a beautiful river. The sun hit it ever so perfectly, creating a beautiful sight for the eyes. It looked like something out of a magazine.

Jimmy and his friends had only done white-water rafting under the supervision of a professional. This was their first time trying it on their own, and they were all excited. Why waste the money at one of those expensive places if you can do it yourself? What could go wrong?

Jimmy chugged a beer and crushed it as he let it out a battle cry and threw the can on the ground. The group got into the raft and away they went, the rough water throwing them around as they drank and had the time of their lives.

Jenny became terrified, thinking they had made a big mistake when she saw the fin. What large fish could be in the river? As Jenny pointed out

A Charity Anthology

something in the distance, Jimmy shrugged it off and Olivia laughed as she took a sip of her wine. Was Jenny just paranoid?

The river got rougher; the waves splashed around. Donny was thrown off the raft and into the water. The raft kept going until they hit a rock that blocked them from going any further upstream. They yelled to Donny to swim to them, but Donny was pulled under by something. Blood gushed out into the stream and all over the group!

Everyone screamed as a great white shark sunk its teeth into the raft. Air was let out as it sank into the river. In a moment's notice, Olivia's head was gone, blood squirting into Jimmy's face as he screamed. Jenny swam away as fast as she could, leaving Jimmy behind. The shark took Jimmy's arm off, chewing on it as Jimmy sank into the water.

Jenny made it to the shore and looked around, the river now filled with blood. She saw no shark, but she knew she was safe on land. Jenny took out her cell phone, but it was just as dead as her friends.

Lost and alone, Jenny walked through the woods until she heard someone screaming. She spotted a car beneath the trees and ran to it. A woman in her thirties lay on the ground, half eaten. A shark on land took a bite out of her dangling intestines. The shark roared at Jenny, and she knew there was no way out. Jenny closed her eyes and soon everything went black.

House Call

Martin W Payne

Sunday, late afternoon in a park. A sunny day making a run pleasant for Katrina, her blonde hair in a ponytail bouncing from side to side behind her. She smiles as she runs around the lake in the centre of the park as a couple of teenage boys play with a remote-control boat. A man with a backpack stands near them but looks at her as she runs past, his eyes following her Lycra clad backside.

A short while later, she runs through a suburban housing estate. Reaching her own house, she opens the front door and steps inside.

Closing the front door, she goes upstairs and returns in loose shorts and a baggy T-shirt. Passing through the living room, she turns the TV on as the news begins and she prepares a quick salad in the kitchen. On the TV the presenter provides a summary of the usual national and international diet of wars, strikes, and rising prices, before starting on the local news.

Katrina returns with her salad bowl and fork and barely sits down before her video doorbell shows a moving image on the TV of a man standing by a car outside her house. Behind the doorbell image, the presenter is talking about the discovery of a woman found dead in her own home. The man in the doorbell video has a backpack on one shoulder and is removing a large black bag out of his car. Katrina frowns and puts the salad bowl down to switch off the TV as the presenter talks about the dead woman being found with no indications of any break-in or, as yet, any cause of death identified.

A Charity Anthology

Katrina opens the front door as the man approaches.

"Can I help you?", she asks.

"Massage for you?" the man replies, showing an ID card with the logo 'massage4u' on it and his picture and name, Dominic Pendragon.

"Oh god, was that tonight? Shit, I thought we said tomorrow!" Katrina exclaims. "Come in!"

"It is still convenient tonight though?" Dominic asks. "Not going out or expecting anyone?"

"No, no, it's all good. Come in, living room is straight though."

"Thanks" he says as he makes his way past her and into the house.

In the living room, he puts his backpack down and unzips the large black bag, removing a portable massage table from it. Setting the table up, he says "Call me Dom, by the way. And remind me, did you want any particular areas worked on?"

"Katrina. And, yes, I just need a deep tissue massage on my left shoulder".

"Great, that's what I recall. If you can just take your T-shirt off and lay on the table, that will be great."

"Cool. You know, I think I've seen you somewhere before," Katrina comments but is just met with a shake of the head from Dominic.

Dominic closes the living room curtains for privacy as Katrina strips off her top, bare torso under it, and lays on the table. Opening his backpack, he removes a small speaker and sets it to play classical music as Katrina relaxes, her face into the hole in the table. He also removes a bottle of massage oil and a pair of tight-fitting surgical style gloves that he pulls over his hands.

"Just relax", he says as he pours a small amount of oil into his gloved hand and then starts to massage her left shoulder. "Hmm, yes, very tense. Do you mind if I just try a small muscle relaxant to help me get the trapezius a bit looser? You know, the shoulder muscle?"

"Sure, if you need to, is it that bad?" Katrina asks.

Dominic grunts in affirmation as he reaches into his backpack and pulls out a small vial and a syringe. Removing the cap from the syringe, he plunges it into the vial and withdraws a full load. The vial is labelled 'curare'. Surprisingly gently, Dominic pricks Katrina's flesh and squeezes the syringe, emptying it into her shoulder, before removing and gently massaging the skin to reduce the very small pinprick and then returning the vial and syringe to his backpack. Removing a box of paper tissues, he starts to remove the oil.

"What are you doing?" Katrina asks.

"Just a relaxant, don't worry. Just close your beautiful eyes. It will be like going to sleep."

Within a minute, her breathing starts to labour as her diaphragm begins to lose power and her lungs fail. The classical music continues as Dominic watches her slip into unconsciousness and then death, filming her final moments on his cell phone.

Gently he picks up her now still body from the massage table and lays her on the sofa. Turning her over, he pulls her shorts down her legs and gently prises open her vagina with his still gloved fingers, filming himself licking her even as her body started to cool, before inserting a finger inside to partially neutralise his own DNA. He takes pictures of her entire nude body on his phone, before pulling her shorts and T-shirt back on, leaving her slumped over on the sofa as though she had just fallen asleep.

Packing up his massage table before turning the music off and closing his backpack, he picks up the remote control, turns the TV back on using Katrina's index finger and allows the remote control to fall onto the floor below her dead right hand.

Making sure nothing has been left behind, Dominic moves to the front door, cautiously opening it with a gloved hand, and shutting it behind him as he leaves. On the TV, the doorbell video shows him in front of the house, removing his gloves, and putting his massage table in his car.

Twenty-four hours later.

The video doorbell again appears on the TV. A man is standing beside a white van with the logo 'massage4U' on the side, removing a black bag similar to the one used by Dominic.

A Return to Light

Cortney Palm

It's midnight. The Grandfather clock performed its ear-rupturing dance of chimes to let me know. I smash the pillow over my head. Just a few days ago my grandma died falling down the stairs. Doc said her bad hip gave out, taking her life in the process. It feels eerie being here. I can still smell the scent of her rose perfume in the air. Now I am here, cleaning out this ancient acropolis, with a hundred years of accumulated junk, until I can put the house on the market.

Anna. What was that? I jump up at the sound of my name. No one is in the house but me. I hold the pillow close to my chest, huddled up against the bed frame as if it will protect me. *Annnnna.* My name stretched out, the voice taunting me.

"Hello?" I call out tentatively. Maybe my mother decided to come after all. But would she sound like that? I ignore my head voice of reason and yell out, "Mom?"

ANNA! This time the voice is terrifying. Demonic. I race to turn on the bedroom light, but I struggle with the knob to turn the lamp on. Oh please, oh please, oh please! The light refuses to come to life. I hunker down next to a stack of boxes and hold my breath. I hear the dreadful sound of heavy footsteps on the staircase just paces away from where I am. I listen carefully. The loud footsteps clunk towards the top of the stairs and onto the landing. I cover my mouth hoping it will silence my fear. My heart thumps hard in my chest. I feel at any moment it will simply explode.

A Charity Anthology

I try to think rationally, can ghosts make sounds? Could this actually just be some regular Joe entering what he thinks is an abandoned house to rob the place? How did he know my name? What did the voice even sound like? It was frightening. A mix of a child, a woman and… and scary demon? Whatever the case, I will not die in fear. I spot a fire poker sticking out of the box. I will fight.

The footsteps stop. I strain to listen. I decide it's time. Wham! I throw open the door and blindly charge out, wielding my fire poker and heading for the stairs! I charge, screaming like a banshee at the top of my lungs, fueling my power and will. I aim the poker for what I hope is the chest of whatever is seeking to kill me, I lunge for it and drive the poker deep into the… air? No one is there!

I fall tumbling down the stairs, falling head over heels. Everything is moving so fast I don't even feel pain. I slam down hard at the bottom of the stairs. My chest feels wet and hot. I can't see a damn thing. My head is ringing. I feel my body lying in a distorted position and I can barely make out the dark red blood staining my favorite white shirt.

I get enough energy to feel my chest. I find the fire poker there, sticking out of my body. I cough up blood. This can't be happening. I start to cry, but oddly enough I don't feel any pain. I hear heels clicking and I manage to turn my head. The lights flicker on to reveal my grandmother staring down at me.

"I want to go home." I choke out the words coated in blood.

"You are home, Anna." She smiles at me. I see a large burnt hand full of boils caress my grandmother's cheek. I shudder at the sight. The hand looks to be steaming as if it's made of smoldering coals. My grandma's smile doesn't fade. I feel an intense fear encompassing me as the entity steps into the light and shows his true form. A menacing monster, a devil in a decrepit human form of burnt flesh.

"Let her go, you monster!" I try to scream but merely whisper as blood fills my throat. Her soul is mine, and yours will be too. This has to be a trick, I think. I move my hands and find my body again. I try to breathe but the pain is too real. I grab the poker with all my might and pull it out of my chest. Blood pours out, free of its hold. I grab the poker and stand up as best I can through the pain, balancing on my one good leg.

You cannot kill me.

"Watch me." I step full force towards the pair, brandishing my weapon in preparation to strike. The demon simply backs away. But I am not aiming for him this time. I look into my grandma's eyes and shove the poker deep into her chest as far as it can go. "I love you Grandma; I wish I would have told you that more often. Return to your light, be free."

NO! I watch as my grandma's form withers away into dust. My eyes are heavy. The blood loss makes it hard for me to see clearly. I feel dizzy and nauseous and collapse onto the hardwood floor. "Go to hell," I muster with the last of my might. The demon seizes and coughs. I squint up at him, my eyes never hurt so bad. I watch as a small blue orb of light exits out of his mouth, followed by another and another. Soon hundreds of little blue orbs escape from this dark mass' mouth. I smile at their freedom. Yet the orbs don't leave, they begin to hover over me but I just can't see anymore. I force a

A Charity Anthology

smile and fade into a serene bliss of blue light. ... Beep. Beep. A soft sound enters my awareness. My eyes flutter open.

"There she is," an angel stands above me smiling. "Welcome back."

The Hair

Tracy Allen

Marissa pulled the makeup mirror even closer to her face, swiveling it up to focus on her eyebrows. The short, black hairs came into focus like a forest of tree trunks growing out of the uneven earth. Without breaking eye contact with the reflective glass, she grabbed her tweezers off the corner of the sink and went to work.

Plucking the first few errant hairs always stung a bit, but after a few good grip and yanks, the endorphins kicked in and Marissa didn't even feel it anymore. The job was mundane and sometimes frustrating, but Marissa would never be caught dead with uneven eyebrows, even if she was just going to work and coming straight home afterwards. You could run into anybody at any time, so it's always best to be ready... makeup light but impeccable, hairstyle held together with just the right amount of control and bounce, a casual outfit that only took three hours to put together, and the slimmest, cutest heels in her closet. Because you never know.

Marissa pulled her head back and compared her two brows. They looked pretty even. One more pluck from the left side and voila! Perfect!

She tilted the mirror once again, this time focusing on the mole. The one imperfection in her face. Sitting just above her upper lip on the right side of her mouth, the small brown dot drew her attention, its single hair like a long, thin spider leg poking out of her face, taking up the entire reflective surface. She regripped the tweezers, grasped the hair at the base, and yanked.

But instead of feeling like a satisfying pinch, the hair almost tickled on its way out. Marissa's perfectly manicured eyebrows furrowed, and she yanked the mirror even closer. Instead of focusing on a dark but supposedly bald bubble of skin, she saw that the hair, that nasty little fucker, was now longer but still attached. She swiped at it with her finger, hoping to wipe it away, but the ugly thing stayed put, now at least half an inch long.

Getting into work on time now forgotten, Marissa wiped her tweezers on a mascara caked tissue and seized the filament. She held her breath and jerked. The weird, tickling sensation returned, and this time, it came with a burning, choking clot in the back of her throat. She dropped the small metal pincers into the sink and gagged, but nothing came out.

"Okay, what the fuck?" she choked, her breath coming in ragged gasps. She caught a glimpse of one of her giant, caricatured eyeballs staring out at her from the round glass's magnified surface, and on instinct, batted the mirror away. It swung into the wall on its thin, segmented arm. "This is crazy. This is crazy, this is crazy, this is crazy... It can't be real."

Taking a deep breath, Marissa pulled the looking glass back toward her face, bracing herself for what the hair must look like now. It was worse than she thought. Laying against her cheek was a long strand of pure black, thicker than normal hair measuring almost an inch and a half. When she moved, the filament waved in the air like a tiny rope, its anchor stuck deep inside her skin.

Without stopping to think about it, Marissa wrapped the hair around her first finger and wrenched her hand away from her body. This time, the suffocating lump became a breathless punch to the back of her throat. She tried to gasp but couldn't draw in a breath. Even after she let go of the hair, the choking mass stuck, blocking off all air. Her lungs burned, and her heart throbbed in her chest. Black spots appeared before her eyes. Her fingers dug at her throat as she tried to open the passageway and draw air. As Marissa's world dimmed, her hand found the black hair, still hanging from her cheek. It was now over a foot long. What it was attached to, she never found out.

Splitting Headache

Jaysen P. Buterin

10:00 PM already?!? Shit.

That meant that he had only had two hours till his deadline. Two hours left to not only finish but to actually even start writing his story for the new *Hot off the Press* anthology. It was his first chance at publication in ages, it was only 1,000 words and it was for charity no less, and here he was with the absolute worst bloody case of writer's block that he'd had in years.

He stared at the painted wooden Elvis clock hanging on the wall, watching the King watch him, hoping for some sort of divine sign that would get him started. He kept trying to convince himself that because it wasn't digital that maybe, just maybe, time wouldn't move as fast. Almost as if the longer he looked at those tarnished analogue hands, the slower the seconds and minutes would tick by. He needed an idea and he needed it now.

His eyes drifted across all the horror movie posters, books, toys and memorabilia that made this 46-year-old man's office look more like a 1980s teenager's clubhouse. Why was this so difficult? He turned his attention back to his very own version of Hell, the 16-inch, 3072 × 1920-pixel prison where the next two hours would feel like a life sentence. The cell that he couldn't escape from, a seemingly innocent, completely blank document just waiting to be filled with chills, thrills and terrors. And on constant patrol was his warden, his guard, his tormentor - the cursor.

He hated that cursor, that smug little blinking

Hot Off the Press

bastard, winking in and out of existence just mocking him. It was as if it was so disappointed in his inability to even articulate a thought that it actually had somewhere else better to be, but it kept coming back just to make sure he still wasn't actually getting anything done. If he could just come up with something, anything, and then out of the blue... the light bulb went off in his head. He had it, he knew what to do! All he had to do was get it out of his head and on the screen and he would feel like a real writer again.

Just as his fingertips touched the keyboard, he felt a sharp stabbing pain behind his right eye. He winced as he sat upright like a spring-loaded action figure, his hands shooting protectively towards both sides of his head. Something wasn't right. He'd had headaches and migraines before, sure, but this was different, this was something... deeper. This hurt, bad. Really bad. Like something was buried in his brain that was now trying to escape. He cried out again as the blinding pain throbbed directly behind both his eyes now, but what really terrified him was that horrible bone-crunching sound he could hear coming from somewhere and getting louder.

The right eye that had been causing him so much pain suddenly popped out of his head onto the desk with a sickening squish. It rolled right past the scrutinizing cursor and plopped onto the floor to become a future cat toy. Howling and growling in guttural pain, his hands went instinctively up to hold his head, which he immediately regretted. If his remaining eye wasn't filling up with blood so fast, it would've been wide as a saucer at feeling a small part of his head moving up and down as if something was poking it... from the inside, like an egg about to hatch.

His entire body jumped up and froze, locked into a shocked state of paralysis. The sickening sound of bone-on-bone breaking now filled the room, as a red hairline crack zigzagged across his forehead. The fracture split further apart, and the blood now began pouring down his body. From the splintering sides of his skull emerged two human fingertips, which quickly turned into four that promptly ripped the entire body down the middle with a stomach-churning sound of wet meat being torn apart. Falling to the floor like a discarded costume, in its place stood something new, its form becoming more human with every brand-new breath it took.

Shaking itself off like a demonic dog after a bloody bath, it slowly sat down at the computer. It looked down to see the bloody halves of the shape it had before… now resting in a growing pool of blood. He sat up straight and shook the cloudiness from his head, along with a chunk or two of the previous owner's skull. He stared at the blank computer screen as a dollop of blood dripped slowly down it. In the blink of a still bloody but blue eye, those oddly familiar fingers of his shot out and started typing the idea that he saw in his head, that he simply *had* to get out.

And not just typing but gliding over the keyboard, dancing as they created sentence after sentence, paragraph after paragraph, page after page, only pausing briefly to brush a piece of brain or gooey bit out of the way. The typing was so supernaturally fast, the words flew onto the screen faster than the accursed cursor could keep up with—almost as if they were afraid to stay inside his head.

Hot Off the Press

He effortlessly finished the story and sent it to the editor with minutes to spare, according to the clock on his computer. *But why stop there?* he thought. He had another idea that he just had to get out, and then another and another! With the same maniacal fervor from before, he kept on typing until he started to feel a slight ache behind his right eye... and from somewhere too close for comfort he started to hear a horrible bone-crunching sound that was vaguely familiar.

A Charity Anthology

No Matter What

Joe Graciano

The wedding was beautiful. All the guests showed up and it blew away the expectations. It all started with simple talks in the beginning. After seeing everything unfold before them, Lawrence and Judy fell in love all over again.

The wedding was simple, with just a handful of people on the grounds of the museum which was closed for their private event. Judy's parents had donated so much money to the arts that they had their own wing. Judy came from money, but never showed it off. She always dressed simply and worked hard, going from uncomplicated retail jobs to college to working in a Fortune 500 company that her family had no connection to. She wanted to show her parents that she was worthy of the family name.

The dinner was catered by the restaurant Lawrence and Judy had their first date at. He whispered into his wife's ear, "This is amazing. I can't believe we got this location."

Judy smiled, "Well, lo and behold, I was lucky that our family friend Martin paid for it. We've known him my whole life. He's practically a father to me."

"I'm sorry your parents couldn't be here," Lawerence said.

Feeling slightly embarrassed, Judy lowered her head and sighed. "They love me, and I love them, but they're just so busy. I know they're proud of us. One day you'll meet them, and when that time comes, we'll all be happy."

Hot Off the Press

Lawerence hugged his wife and held her. Judy leaned into the sweet embrace, and she hugged her new husband in a tight squeeze. The rest of the night consisted of dancing, laughing, and love.

As time went by, the newlyweds experienced the same thing that other couples go through with work, life, and trying to find time for each other. Judy was now busy working a simple 9-5 job while Lawerence worked extra hard to be the main breadwinner of the house.

Suddenly, the new husband found himself ill. He was unable to work and became hospitalized, which wiped out their savings. Judy tried her hardest to keep their little family afloat, even going to the extreme of selling clothes, furniture, and anything else in their house.

"I love you, no matter what you look like," she would tell her husband. One day, Judy arrived at the hospital wearing a scarf around her head and sunglasses. She explained, "I sold my hair to a store and got some more money for us. With makeup, I can probably be on Svengoolie show now," she laughed.

As time went on, Lawrence grew sicker and money became tighter. He had to move back into their house where he was able to earn a bit of money. However, working at home for a few hours was all he could muster. From living a lavish style to their now poverty-based lives was the new norm. Judy did all the hard work, and she looked haggard and tired. Lawrence would just smile at her and say, "I love you, no matter what."

The disease grew stronger, leaving Lawrence bedridden, a former shell of who he once was. He woke up one night to the sound of Judy's voice.

A Charity Anthology

"It's finally time for you to meet Mama and Daddy," she said. "I worked so hard, and now, they finally see me for who I am. Their lifeblood." A beeping, clicking machine was wheeled into the room, and attached to it was Judy... but not all of her. Just her head, which was nestled in a jar. "I was working all this time, yes. Working the family business. See, we realized that the key to life is to get rid of our bodies and organs. We sell them and then collect vast fortunes."

Judy wheeling herself closer to Lawrence. He tried to scream but was too weak. Two more carts with heads in glass jars rolled in. They were Judy's parents, covered in liver spots and balding, their exposed jaws smiling at their son-in-law. Family friend Martin followed close behind, dressed in scrubs and holding a whirring electric saw.

"Welcome to the family!" He smiled as he put on his surgical mask.

A Piece of You

Nat Whiston

He didn't even wake up, although with the amount he drank with those sleeping pills I'm not surprised. I'm standing here trying to figure out if there was any point in bringing the chloroform. But then again, I do not want this guy waking up during the process. I move close to his armchair, I'm right behind him now. Hovering just in front of his face is the soaked rag, my other arm ready at the side in case I need to put him in a chokehold. It would be easier if he was dead, but I need him alive. For now.

I knew that I had to check everything was in working order, wouldn't just yank the damn thing out without checking. I managed to get some surgical equipment off a certain website that pretty much stocks all your needs in once place. I pull out the needle from my carrier bag and push the point through the seal, sucking in the clear liquid till it reached the level on the gauge.

The stuff I start injecting into his neck isn't aesthetic. Oh no, he didn't deserve to be let off that easy.

I brought this stuff from a guy that owes me a favour, with interest. Johnny, we will call him, saved me a bottle of Mivacurium that he lifted from his last clinic break in. Told me that this is a strong neuromuscular blockade, should keep our boy Terry here nice a paralysed so I can check the merchandise. I'm not sure how much I'm supposed to give him, but hey, I'm no doctor. A little should go a long way, according to Johnny.

Now it's time to make the first incision, I bring

A Charity Anthology

out my pen knife. Clean of course, all my kit has been through intense cleaning with alcohol beforehand, I press the blade to the centre of his chest and slide the blade down firmly. My packet of gauze is at the ready, as the blood starts to trickle out of the wound as it starts to get wider. The bastard's a bleeder, should have expected it really with the amount of alcohol in his system. It's bound to thin the blood, making things messy for me as the blood cascades down his beer gut. I have a nice wide wound now, so I carry on carefully cutting until I hit bone. I saw the medical videos on YouTube so I'm pretty sure I can follow them correctly. I mean, I managed to fix my washing machine issue thanks to videos online so why not an amateur surgery. God, there is way more blood than I expected but his sternum is now completely visible. Now the hard part, I couldn't get a chest separator online, so I decided to improvise a little.

I drop the pen knife and reach into my bag for the large pair of bolt cutters. I'm hoping if they cut through metal then bone will be a piece of piss. I lock the jaws around the chunky centre bone, two deep breaths then I put on the pressure, it may not take two attempts after all. Once sharp snap and the first cut is done. Once more and I can move the piece of chest bone out of the way to get to the treasure beneath.

SNAP!

Perfect, it sounds like when I break into a chicken carcass. His eyes shoot open and scare the crap out of me, but as he looks at me with eyes full of fear, I just can't help myself.

"Hi Terry, you are *finally* awake," I coo, panic in his eyes as they shoot around the room. His face is unable to move or show emotion but I know he is screaming internally.

I carry on with the task at hand and move the tissue blocking my view. There it is, pumping away frantically. The heart is thumping at a hundred beats per minute, even with abuse it has suffered over the years. It still looks healthy. I check for abrasions and darkening but find no issues anywhere on this powerful and valuable muscle, well, valuable to me maybe, certainly not him. I look up at him and smile wickedly, as horror forces his pupils to dilate when I reach inside the cavity I have created. One hard yank, and Terry passes away before the last beat of his heart. The worthless waste of life lies still, a corpse before the heart even leaves his body. I stretch down my gloved hands to the picnic container and lift the latch with one, the other still wrapped around my gift. I place it carefully in the ice, worried my rageful action of tearing it out may have damaged it in some way.

Once I've cleaned up, I'll head to the hospital to see her - we have been waiting three months for a heart transplant for Lucy. The only relative with a matching blood type was Terry. I close the lid of the box and start packing away my things, glancing over at the pathetic waste that used to be my brother.

We noticed a change in Lucy a couple of months ago, she suddenly closed off on us, and we knew having a bad heart wasn't the only thing on her mind. It was only ever when she came back after staying here, in this place with him. When she finally told me, I felt sick to my stomach. Even now looking at him turns my stomach. Lucy only asked one thing of me. She said, "Daddy, when I get

A Charity Anthology

better, I don't want to stay over at Uncle Terry's anymore."

I rise to my feet, fighting back the tears. I have to be strong; my baby needs me, and I have to bring her this brand-new heart.

"Don't worry honey, Daddy won't let Uncle Terry hurt you ever again."

The Rise of the Scarecrows

Callum Pearce

"Just pull up over here," Sam asked her brother.

"You said you wanted a lift to the bar, I'm not stopping off everywhere on the way," John snapped.

"I just want to leave some flowers for that poor kid." Sam reached into the back seat for the bunch of roses she had put there earlier. She climbed out of the car and waited for a moment but her brother made no move to join her. "Are you coming with me? It's dark out here, anything could happen," she shouted into the vehicle.

"I don't know why you need to do this, you didn't even know the fella." John seemed annoyed but also a little scared. He knew however that he would never hear the end of it if he didn't do what his sister wanted. "I can't believe you've got me traipsing through muddy fields at night to leave flowers for some queer you didn't even know."

"Don't use words like that, especially here," Sam complained. "He was an innocent kid who was killed for being gay. They sprayed that disgusting word on the tree they left his body leaning against."

They trudged through the farmer's field to a large tree. It was surrounded by flowers, toys and photos of the young man who had been found there. The bark had been scraped off where the killers had sprayed their hateful signature. After placing the flowers, Sam wandered over to the tatty-looking scarecrow that stood nearby. John stomped along behind her, his feet squelching in the wet, muddy ground.

"That's what they said he looked like," Sam said,

A Charity Anthology

gesturing to the scarecrow. "It was all over the headlines. The people that found him said that he was so badly beaten that he was unrecognisable as a human. Even when they got closer, they thought they were looking at a scarecrow. Unfinished and left leaning against the tree until the farmer returns to raise it to the cross."

"I don't see why it bothers you so much. That kid was always asking for trouble. Flouncing around town in makeup, holding hands with his boyfriends and shoving his queerness down everybody's throat," John ranted.

"I don't know why his sexuality bothers you so much," Sam mumbled.

"It doesn't, but this is Wigan. If you walk around like that, you're bound to draw attention to yourself. Why are you acting like he was your best friend all of a sudden anyway? You didn't know him any more than anyone else you pass in a bar once in a while."

"I know him now," Sam began. "I came here last week after hearing about it on the news. I left a bunch of mixed flowers but he told me roses were his favourite. I had to come back to deliver those."

"What are you going on about now? You sound insane," John growled.

"He showed me everything." She reached out and took the scarecrow's hand. "He showed me what it was like to walk through this town seeing the looks of disgust that were aimed at him every day. He showed me that same look on the faces of his own family. He even showed me you and David following him home from the bar that night.

"I wasn't just here to deliver the roses," Sam smiled. "I came here to deliver you."

Hot Off the Press

The scarecrow's head lolled to one side and the cloth that had been covering it fell away. John remembered the face that he was looking at now very well. Swollen and bruised, covered in dried blood, dark like tar. Two clean lines were running from the corner of the eyes to its chin. John had been quite proud of his work on that night but now he was terrified. The thing raised its head and forced open the eyes that had been sealed shut with blood. It grinned, showing the teeth that John had broken with his baseball bat.

"You brought the spray paint with you, you brought weapons. You and David planned this. You set out that night to do this to an innocent kid." Tears were running down Sam's face like they had the boy's on that night.

John tried to turn and get away but his feet had been slowly sinking into the mud. As he tried to pull them out, the mud sucked harder.

"You're his now," Sam cried.

John started wheezing and coughing. He wriggled and jerked, trying to free himself from the mud. Reaching to his mouth he started pulling clumps of straw out and throwing them to the floor.

"...your brother..." he managed to wheeze as straw started to fill his stomach and throat.

"He let me see you through his eyes. That was not my brother, that was a monster filled with hate and rage," Sam said, then turned and started walking away.

John could feel the straw pushing from his stomach into his arms. It ripped through his flesh and blocked any oxygen from entering his lungs. It pushed through his skull and hung around his head like a tatty wig. The pain was unbearable and never-ending. His arms stood out at each side, stiff. John stayed staring into the face of his victim forever.

Scarecrows started appearing all over England. People tried to burn them, demolish them, throw them into lakes. Every single one returned to the spot it had first been found. Nobody knew where they came from. Sam suspected these were other young people like her scarecrow. Kids that never made the headlines but suffered the same. She imagined this boy's pain and sorrow had lit a path for all of them, bringing them home. Gradually, each scarecrow grew its little family. They took the hate-filled creatures that had created them or other monsters that nurtured that same rage inside them. Every time Sam read about another scarecrow appearing somewhere, she shed a tear. Each one was a symbol of the hatred and cruelty that existed around her.

The Promise

Kenn Hoekstra

Cole dropped a single ice cube into a rocks glass and filled it with three fingers of Booker's. Make that four. His hand trembled and his throat burned as he gulped the liquor down. Anya's funeral had rattled him more than he had anticipated. He hoped the bourbon would help put his mind at ease.

Cole took a deep breath, set the glass down on the end table, and loosened his tie. He walked to the gun cabinet, slid the ornate, wooden door aside, and grabbed his father's double-barrelled shotgun. Cradling the weapon in his arms, he fished a couple of shells out of the cardboard box on the top shelf and chambered them. He placed a couple more shells in his breast pocket before snapping the breach shut.

He walked over to the rocking chair in the corner, pulled it out to the center of the room, spinning it around to face the front door. Cole sat down in the chair, rested the shotgun in his lap, leaned back, and lit a cigarette. He closed his eyes and felt a wave of calm wash over him.

Anya, his wife of thirteen years... thirteen long, miserable years...was dead. Gone. He had made it look like an accident. No one suspected a thing. Not the police. Not her friends. Not even her parents, who had hated him with a passion for as long as he could remember. His grieving widower act was convincing. It had to be. He even managed to produce some tears at this afternoon's service.

He had done it. He was finally free.

There was just one small problem. The fall didn't

kill her. Not instantly, anyway. She saw what he did, and despite her shattered neck and spine, her fiery gaze seared his very soul. He couldn't escape that horrific, almost demonic stare. He could only stand there, frozen, and watch as the last vestiges of life drained from her broken body. With seething hatred, she cursed him with her dying breath.

He requested a closed casket. "Her wishes," he told the mortician. Cole couldn't bear the thought of looking at her one moment longer.

Cole felt the icy grip of terror crush his newfound serenity. Was that scratching he heard when he threw in the first handful of dirt? It was, wasn't it? There was no doubt in his mind: she was coming back for him. She promised. It was just a matter of time.

Cole looked at his watch. How long would it take, he wondered? To escape the coffin? To claw through that fresh earth? The cemetery's a good hour's walk from here. Or would she have to crawl? Damn.

Cole took a long drag from his cigarette, stubbed it out, and adjusted the shotgun in his lap. No, it wouldn't be long now. Anya was never one to keep him waiting.

The Executioners

Dineta Williams-Trigg

They both had been hiding in plain sight. Presenting themselves as "normal humans" had been easier than they had anticipated. Normal humans, HA! That was a misnomer, for the cruelty that humans visited on to one another knew no bounds. She never felt guilty when she had to kill one or two of them, it was so easy.

He had always left their bodies intact after feeding on them so delicately. Often jokingly, she would offer him a knife and a napkin to make his meal more enjoyable. They had argued about it many times.

"We are better than them," he would say.

"They don't deserve our empathy," she would reply, and she would always win the debate. She had started being creative with her kills, becoming bored with the simple stab and slash method they had been taught so long ago. She had begun ripping and tearing at their soft bodies. Feeling the warm blood run down her face as she tore out throats and stomachs. Occasionally, she chewed on damaged fingers if they got close enough to her teeth. That final satisfactory crunching sound of their larynx as they stopped fighting her and lay still, their life blood still gushing from the holes in their bodies. Damn, it was delicious!

Ever the performer, she would always make a show of slurping loudly and chewing slowly, taking her time, because she knew that it pissed him off. Using whatever victim's coat sleeve she was wearing to wipe her face, then burping when she was finished, dried blood covering her from head to toe. He would just stand silently by and listen to their screams, deep down inside knowing that she was right, they deserved no mercy.

Every town and every place would end the same. She poured the gasoline, and he lit the match. It felt good to watch the town burn. Time and time again, humans had been warned "To be better, don't fuck with the planet or with each other." But for centuries they had failed. Their screams floated up into the night sky. Other beings joined the circle to celebrate and dance, knowing that they were now free of this forsaken place and that they would be allowed to move on.

She looks at him, noticing how his eyes shimmer in the flames. He sees her watching him, they clasp hands and retreat into the darkness, for there were other places to burn and destroy, because they were coming, she and him, they were the judge and jury, the Earth's executioners. The day of reckoning, their judgement day was upon them.

Thoughts on Visiting the Man with the Hood

Rollin Jewett

Nothing has changed. The walls are black and dark. The rats are there. The water drips. The smell is dank and moldy. The walls are too smooth to climb. What the hell am I doing here? My three buddies are still...wait a minute...three buddies...?

Now there's only two! I guess they got another one. The man with the hood has been pretty busy lately. They must've come in while I was sleeping and dragged the poor bastard out. I thought I heard someone screaming in my sleep. Or was I awake? Who knows? It all seems the same, this hellish nightmare.

There's only two now...plus me. I've lost track of time since I got here, but there were several of us before. I still don't know why I'm in here. I guess I did something that was a no-no.

Jeez, this place smells. Death himself must smell like this. I wonder how long I've been here? Days? Weeks? Who the hell knows? I wish I could see my face. It feels rough. Scabby. And Christ, I need a shave! They say they're going to set me free soon. I don't make much noise and I don't eat much. Ever eat a fried rat? I don't think you'd eat much either.

My two buddies are...what the hell? Now there's only one! They aren't wasting any time, are they? My other buddy's white as a ghost now. His eyes are bulging with fear and he's moaning like a kicked dog. He says he's hungry. The guard outside the cell says he won't have to wait long. I hope today's rat tastes better than yesterday's. Maybe they'll put some gravy on it for his last meal -- make it

A Charity Anthology

gourmet.

I shouldn't make fun of him. He's probably very nice. On the other hand, he's in here for murder. Most of us are. I hope I'm not. I can't remember. I don't think I am or else they wouldn't say they're gonna set me free soon. They usually take someone out to see the man with the hood once a day. I don't know whether a day has passed but...now there's only me!

I heard some vague screams a while ago -- like through a cloudy tunnel. Besides the usual voices, of course. The ones that are always raging at me. I sort of remember them trying to take my buddy out. He yelled for them to take me instead and grabbed my leg -- trying to pull me out with him! I remember kicking him hard in the face. His forehead opened up and gushed a crimson stream. I guess I was mad at him. I'm not now, though.

I hope they hang him from the sun.

I'm all alone now. I don't have anyone to talk to. Shut up! Maybe I'm going mad. I wonder if I am. That would be unfortunate at this point. So close to my release. Now the rats are starting to laugh at me. Again. They think it's hilarious. Shut up! Shut the hell up, damn you! I'll kill you, eat you raw! Then who'd be laughing?

I'm not scared of the man with the hood. They said I'm going to be free. They promised. Oh, why did they leave me in here? Saving the best for last? That must be it. I must be the best. At what, though? Murder?

Here they come, all dressed in black. They've grabbed my arms and they're pulling me to my feet. I'm too weak to fight back. There are too many.

Hot Off the Press

They're too strong. Are they going to set me free now? They're unshackling me. The sound of rattling chains is deafening.

I still hear the rats -- with their shrill laughter. I'd kill them all, every last one of them if I could only get my hands around their tiny throats. Tiny throats?

Babies... I remember babies. Crying and screaming all the time. Enough to drive you insane. Why did they have to do that? But I fixed it. I made them all be quiet. They're all asleep now.

They're closing the door behind us. Goodbye home, sweet home. I can still hear those stupid rats laughing, telling jokes – mocking me. But I'll have the last laugh soon... when I'm free.

We're walking down a long hallway. I can feel the guard's hands on me, but I can't see them. It's too dark.

Now we're outside. I shield my eyes from the sun. They're leading me up some stairs. There's a huge crowd below the platform. I see some people smiling at me, laughing. Some are applauding. I stifle an urge to bow. I guess they know I'm going to be free.

They're putting something around my neck. A medal?

I'm a hero!

I see the man with the hood. What's he doing at my party? Who invited him? He's not smiling or clapping. Party pooper. He's touching something. The crowd's cheering. I'm falling!

Ahhhhhh... free at last.

It's What's Inside that Counts

Lindsey Ellis-Holloway

The room was *filled* with paraphernalia.

Posters, plushies, action figures, lunch boxes, pencil cases, books and t-shirts of all shapes, sizes, ages and conditions. Some looked like absolute junk, some were in pristine condition, but all were clearly loved by their current owner regardless. It was obvious that a pretty penny had been spent accumulating the extensive collection.

Alongside the official merchandise—displayed with as much love and pride as the objects bought and paid for—were a myriad of hand-drawn pictures, clay models and homemade costumes depicting the same character that lined every surface the eye could see. Even the bedspread was covered in the image of the somewhat demented-looking TV character, its purple face with its inane grin staring lifelessly at the ceiling from one side of the bedroom.

Tommy loved every last object, no matter how small or tattered or common it may be. His more rare and expensive pieces were stored carefully in their glass cases; removed only when he wore his gloves to clean them before they were placed tenderly in their places where he could look at them all day.

There was one piece that Tommy loved more than anything else in the world, something only *he* owned. A life-size cut out of his idol, with an autograph across the chest. The last of its kind, he'd made sure of that, though it had taken him *years* to get rid of the others out there. When the last of the

Hot Off the Press

cardboard cut-outs had been burnt to ashes it had been big news on the forums, and when the TV show was finally cancelled the news crews had descended upon Tommy's room to interview him. They all wanted to know what *YaYa YoYo Go Go Gi*'s biggest fan thought about the show finally ending.

It had been the worst day of Tommy's life, finding out there would be no more episodes and no further merchandise to buy, but it had been the *greatest* day having the news crew come into his room to see the splendour of everything only *he* owned. The reporter said his room was like a museum, a real tribute to the age of YaYa and everything that the show embodied over the last two decades. When they'd left, the forums had blown up over the interview but their hype about his collection soon dwindled, as did memories of Tommy's beloved idol. All he was, his room and his things, even the re-runs on VHS and DVD, weren't enough to fill the hole the show left in his life. Tommy felt alone.

Until now.

After two years of research, and another six months of bribing and begging various channels in the TV business, *finally* Tommy had the name and number of the man he most wanted to meet in the world. The out-of-work actor hadn't needed much persuading to do a private appearance as his once beloved character. The money Tommy offered was more than the man would have accepted at this point, but Tommy would have given his left arm to see YaYa in the flesh at last.

Literally.

Tommy clapped his hands happily, his maniacal

grin reflected back at him in the blank plastic eyes of the costume's head. YaYa had always looked so alive on screen, but now he was sitting in Tommy's room, tied to the chair, he looked... empty. Tommy scowled and poked the lolling head of the costume, anger rising in his chest as the innards of the costume gave a groggy groan.

He stomped his feet as he moved over to the desk where all his art supplies, dirty with paint and clay from his own personal art projects, lay strewn across its surface. He moved the tools about until he found his clay knife, hammer and chisel. The groggy, costumed figure saw the implements and whimpered.

"Let me go!" the muffled voice demanded, though it seemed half-hearted from within the lifeless head of the costume.

"No. You're mine now. All mine. And soon I'm going to wear your skin and I'll be with YaYa forever!" Tommy replied gleefully.

"What?! No! No! Let me go, you psychopath!" the man inside the costume squealed.

Tommy grinned at his reflection in YaYa's plastic eyes as he pressed a foot to YaYa's fluffy purple chest, pushing him over in the chair. The man squealed as the chair tipped and he ended up on his back, the chair splintering on impact and freeing him of his bonds. Though he still didn't stand a chance.

Before 'YaYa' could understand that he was free, Tommy was on top of him, squealing in delight as he brought down the clay knife into the space between where the head sat and the costume zipped up on the torso. Blood poured over Tommy's hands and the man inside the outfit gargled and choked as the thick liquid filled his mouth and throat, drowning him with each desperate, pointless gasp for breath.

Tommy never hesitated, using the knife to slice through costume and flesh as if they were one and the same. Before long the thrashing stopped, and Tommy tore open the wound he'd made, lifting chisel and hammer to the exposed rib cage beneath the blood and gore. Tommy brought the hammer down upon the chisel, shivering with pleasure at the crack as bone gave way beneath the force of his strike. He hit again, and again, and again until every rib was snapped, allowing him to remove the chest plate to reveal the gooey insides within.

"I always wanted to know what you looked like on the inside," Tommy giggled, diving elbow deep into the man's chest cavity, while YaYa's dead eyes stared back at him.

Beastiary

MJ Dixon

The man, hungry, exhausted, wounded from battle had come across the old shack deep in the woods. It was dark as he broke down the door, desperate and hoping for a place to take shelter. When the old man inside attacked, he had no choice but to defend himself, to kill the man.

As he died, he whispered, "It is yours now."

Then, he found the man's daughter, chained up, used as bait every night, holding an old, tattered book, a glossary of deadly creatures, and how to kill them.

The old man protected the world from these beasts as the night came, now it must fall to him, as inhuman screaming erupted from the woods and the monstrous shadows moved in.

Casey

James Jobling

HOME

Using a branch for a crutch, I saunter barefoot along the scorched road; shocked but elated to see the thatched cottages of Garland still standing; blackened by fire, humbled by war, but defiant in their unyielding resolve. Most of the windows are shattered, and wispy smoke hovers above the crippled village like a grey blanket – a blanket which poisons my lungs and makes me vomit bloody gruel.

I am dying. Nothing can stop that. Exposure to radiation was unavoidable wandering the aftermath. I don't care, so long as I draw my final breath holding Casey. Her love is the only thing that kept me going these last three days.

Ghostly faces appear in the cavities of houses, my revulsion mirrored in their glazed eyes. Regardless of being one of their own, the villagers fear me. I don't blame them. In my current state, I must resemble a harbinger of death; my body is blistered with third-degree burns, tattered clothes melted to skin, the majority of my hair – and teeth – lost to radiation poisoning. The painful wails of distressed mothers and petrified children ring out all around the village, bullet holes piercing many of the sagging structures. Further along the road, I struggle upon a crater venting ash. A two-inch carpet of nuclear fallout covers Garland in a sooty embrace.

Casey.

I wish I had been with my wife when the bombs started to drop. London, Edinburgh, Manchester,

A Charity Anthology

Glasgow, Birmingham, Cardiff – they have all been reduced to smouldering rubble. It was only a matter of time before the deranged bastard pushed that big red button. He threatened it enough times, but the media always played it down for fear of mass panic. I am – or *was* – a financier who was attending a conference when the four-minute warning siren tooted. Christ, it was like nothing I have ever heard before – or wish to again. Fortunately, the bank holding the convocation had a vault where the staff and I sought shelter from the detonation.

The iron gate droops lopsided on its hinges and, nudging it open, I painfully ascend a footpath of rusty fencing, parched grass, and stacked sandbags to mine and Casey's cottage. All I can think about is holding her again. All the horror I have witnessed, all the sickness I have inherited, all the trauma inflicted upon me, I know Casey's warmth will kiss those bruises away.

The front door has been blown off its pivots but, with great effort, I enter the house and find framed photographs of a pre-existent world still surprisingly affixed to smoke-damaged walls, skewered but otherwise intact - a window into times of past. A black-and-white photograph of Casey and I in a meadow on our wedding day, birthdays, Christmases, wisps of sadness, hints of hard times to come… the storms I have navigated and won. I continue down the hall and stagger into the lounge, smiling when I see Casey standing over the fireplace.

"Casey, baby." The words burn my suppurated throat. "I'm home." I shuffle towards her, holding my arms out to embrace her. "I'm sorry I took so long."

She doesn't reply.

"They did it. Can you believe that? They really did it." Tenderly, I lift the brass urn from the mantelpiece and collapse into the only armchair, hugging the cistern to my chest. "The mad bastard really did it."

Breast cancer claimed Casey three years ago, not nuclear fucking warheads, and I am glad she never saw what was to become of her green and pleasant countryside – or the destruction man was capable – and *willing* – to impose on each other.

Dredging the drawer of the bureau reveals a full bottle of sleeping pills, and I take them one-by-one, holding Casey to my aching heart until the room spins and my eyelids droop

Briefly, from far away, I hear an air raid siren foretell more death and destruction, but it disturbs my slumber very little as the world turns black and I drift towards my Casey…

A Charity Anthology

Lake Woodboard

Reyna Young

Caroline and her boyfriend Greg decided to take a last-minute camping trip to Lake Woodboard. It wasn't too far, just a town over and a place they hadn't camped at yet. It took them almost four and a half hours to drive there, but they thought it was well worth it for a lovely quiet weekend alone. They hadn't been able to spend much time together since Greg's promotion. Nowadays, all he does is work, work, and work. What they didn't know was that the sign for Lake Woodboard lay on the ground with graffiti written over it which read HAUNTED WOODS.

Once there, Caroline began unpacking things and double-checking she brought everything they needed; Greg set up the tent, which took a while due to him trying to remember how to do it. But once he had it up, they started a night of relaxing under the stars. They liked how it was more than just peaceful; no one else was around. They figured being a Friday night, it would have been a little crowded, but the campground belonged to only them, much to their surprise.

They talked for hours, finally catching up with what one another were up to. Between their jobs and trying to find time for one another, plus making time for themselves, it was nice to finally see one other in person rather than over the phone or text. Caroline had done her best to make sure she was available every night before bed to talk to him, even with her busy schedule as well.

They were so wrapped up in each other's

Hot Off the Press

conversation that they never noticed someone watching them from afar. This mysterious person happened to be standing behind a tree for the last two hours. Even with the fire Greg had going it was so dark out there this person was not seen at all. Standing there unseen made this mysterious person smile... smile at the fact they had no idea he was out there. Soon enough he would have two more friends joining him in the woods – forever.

Caroline went through her purse to look for some chapstick after Greg walked off to relieve himself. As she looked, she heard a branch break from behind her. She turned, peering around at the woods. She couldn't see much at all but was hoping that it was a small animal and not a bear. She's seen so many videos of bear encounters while camping it kind of scared her to go back to the woods.

She shrugged off the sound and continued looking for her chapstick. When she finally found it, she heard another noise from behind her. She jumped up, immediately looking around again; this time she was getting scared. The hairs on her arms began to rise, she was getting goosebumps, and the feeling of being watched crossed her mind. Maybe it was an animal or maybe it was something else, either way her imagination was spinning.

"Greg!" she called out to him nervously.

But there was no answer; she walked over toward where he had gone and looked around the area. "Greg!" She called out to him once again but a little quieter. Her stomach began to turn over the silence he was giving her. She wasn't sure what to think as he wouldn't pull a prank like this on her; he knows she scares easily and hates it.

She called out to him again but this time a little

A Charity Anthology

louder, and when she didn't hear back, the rustling of a bush nearby began to shake, causing her to step back.

"Oh no!" she whispered, thinking that maybe an animal would jump out. Greg jumped out of the woods, scaring her. She hit him on the shoulder, pissed off he did that. He told her he saw something and that she needs to see it too.

They walked into the woods. Being very careful not to fall over anything, they walked quite a way from their campsite. She realized that with how far he had walked off it's no wonder he hadn't heard her calling for him. He pointed over to a tall thick tree that had the word "Leave" carved on it. She felt uncomfortable and walked back to their fire, only to find her purse on the floor and all her belongings scattered about. Greg helped her pick her things up and explained it must have been the wind, but she was convinced something else was going on.

They let the fire burn out on its own as they cuddled up in their tent; she was exhausted but couldn't get what was carved on that tree out of her head. On the other hand, Greg thought nothing of it and fell asleep. As soon as Caroline began to drift off, the sound of branches breaking around their tent began.

Caroline's eyes opened; the noise sounded like multiple people walking around their tent, snapping tiny branches under their feet. Caroline sat up and looked around to see shadowy figures walking outside their tent; she pushed Greg to wake him, but he was deeply asleep. She pushed him repeatedly until he opened his eyes and let him know someone was out there. Greg looked over to see the silhouette of someone outside their tent, just standing there.

Hot Off the Press

He put his finger up to her lips for her to stay quiet. A few minutes passed, and the noise and silhouette disappeared. Greg threw his shoes on, grabbed the flashlight, and headed out of the tent, despite her telling him not to. She sat there waiting for his return, but he took so long that she decided to check on him.

She didn't want to attract attention by calling out his name, so she flashed the light around instead. The light bounced off Greg's shoe lying there on the ground. Caroline slapped her hand over her mouth to stop herself from screaming. She flashed the light around to find his other shoe and then his flashlight on the ground. She ran over and picked it up... Greg wasn't around.

Tears began to run down her cheeks; she couldn't believe what she was staring at. She turned, flashing her light around the darkened woods. She didn't know what to do, so she began screaming Greg's name out, hoping he would respond, hoping he was still around and still alive.

As she yelled his name out, she heard a noise from behind her; she turned around to see someone standing near their tent. She squinted her eyes to see the blue and white pattern of Greg's button-down checkered shirt.

In a smiling relief, she ran over. "Greg!" she yelled out again. She thought he must have been looking for her and that's why he was standing there, but as she got closer, she saw he didn't look the same. He was paler, his eyes were pitch black and a grin wouldn't leave his face. Caroline screamed but no one was around to hear her cries.

Greg and Caroline were never seen again.

Night Drive

Melanie Vukusich

The gas station was empty when Marion filled up her tank. The coffee machine was out of order; she bought the next best thing to stay awake: chocolate-covered espresso beans. On her way out, she texted her roommate where she was, despite the late hour.

There were few other vehicles on the road. Staying in the fast lane to avoid the lane change dance, ever so often, a car would appear right behind her as if by magic. Then, she'd change lanes, watching the red glow of the taillights fade into the gaping black maw of the moonless desert night.

Marion's eyes were tired. The bright white lane lines blurred. She turned up her favorite paranormal AM radio show and popped more espresso beans in her mouth. They were gritty and bitter but forced her eyes open for bits of time.

An hour down the road, she realized she hadn't seen any other cars for a while. That made her feel alone, nervous. Her eyes were tired again. Burned out on espresso beans, she rolled down her window. Surely the shock of hot, loud air on her face would stir her. Slightly rejuvenated, Marion increased her speed. She was looking forward to a shower and her own bed.

A sudden rustling in the passenger seat belatedly reminded Marion about the grocery bag sitting there, full of snack wrappers, tissues, and empty water bottles. The wind streaming into the car caught the bag. Keeping her left hand on the steering wheel, Marion attempted to catch the trash that longed to escape her vehicle. Peeling her eyes

Hot Off the Press

from the black desert road, she grabbed at the grocery bag. Suddenly, it flew into the night, a pale plastic ghost on the wind.

"Dammit!" Marion punched the steering wheel. She hated littering. She hated feeling out of control. She hated that she was so far away from home. Lost in her angry thoughts about sleep deprivation, Marion did not see the pale, gaunt figure standing on the roadside, watching her vehicle with intent.

Forty minutes later, Marion was listening to loud music and making herself dance in the driver's seat to keep herself awake. One of her favorite songs from the '90s came on and she was actually enjoying herself, feeling silly and nostalgic.

Thunk. Immediately her low tire pressure indicator light came on. The car swerved a little as Marion righted it and pulled off the road into the dirt. If the tire wasn't in too bad of shape, she would make it to the travel center fifteen minutes down the road.

Retrieving her flashlight from the glovebox, she ascertained movement out in the desert beyond. "It's probably a coyote," Marion rationalized out loud. "Aha!" Flashlight in hand, she exited the vehicle. The desert floor crunched underfoot as she walked to the passenger side. Shining the light in the distance, all she saw were desert scrubs and a four-foot-tall fence running parallel to the road. Examining the tire, a jagged gash missed the sidewall. Marion groaned and looked for her Fix-a-Flat. It wasn't the best option but would have to do. She'd go slow down the highway.

Looking out into the night, Marion heard footsteps just beyond the fence. Whipping around, her flashlight revealed nothing. "My mind is playing tricks on me," she said to herself, only partially convinced. With her tire patched, Marion got back into the vehicle. She'd pulled up too close to some large rocks. Shifting into reverse, the backup camera turned on. On the screen, two pale legs stalked closer and closer to the back of her car. Marion looked in her rear-view mirror. Her blood ran cold. A grey face, with a ridiculously wide red mouth and luminous, deep-set eyes peered in through her back window.

"Shit!" Marion locked the doors. It knew it had been spotted. It began to climb up the back of the car. Sending out a silent prayer, Marion stepped on the gas. The vehicle jerked back, throwing it to the ground. Frantically switching gears to get back on the road, Marion saw it stand up and hiss at her, revealing rows of jagged teeth.

She tried to take it slowly. As the passenger side tire went up onto the asphalt, a swift exit became impossible. "No!" she screamed, beginning to cry. The vehicle lurched sideways as the creature threw itself on top of the car. Filled with adrenaline, her flight response got the better of her and she ran out into the highway. Hissing again, the creature jumped into the road and followed. Marion felt something cold grab her ankle; down she went, hitting her chin on the road. Her blood glistened in a thin trail across the asphalt as the creature dragged her back to the side of the road. Turning to look at it, she was assaulted by an unearthly, high-pitched scream. The creature was content with its prize.

Marion found herself in a precarious place. She teetered between giving up and surviving. She made a decision. Pulling the leg the creature was holding to draw it in, Marion kicked with her other leg, landing a blow to the side of the creature's head. It hissed and let go. She got up and ran across the highway, noticing headlights for the first time in a while. Running through the dirt median, the creature was mere feet behind her.

The approaching vehicle was closer now, hurtling down on them. Marion stepped out onto the road, looking back. The creature was no longer there. A hiss caught her attention. It'd jumped in front of her, landing on the highway. It crouched, jumping to take her down once and for all. Paralyzed, Marion barely processed the creature, the heavy wet *smack* as a semi-truck barreled into it at eighty miles per hour. Gore littered the road. On autopilot, Marion walked back across the median, spotting what in her heart, she knew to be the creature's family. She sighed.

Meth Gator: The Dealer

John Shatzer

Scooter pushes the long greasy blonde hair back from his face before securing it under the grubby stained Budweiser cap holding it in place. Wiping at his sweaty face with a grimy rag, he sighs before continuing down the humid concrete tunnel.

"Damn cops," he curses while slogging through the knee depth stagnant brown water, some of which spills over the top of his ragged looking rubber boots further soaking his already sodden socks and feet.

When the sheriff's office had started raiding the labs around the county, Scooter had packed up his supply of meth and stashed it in the runoff tunnels. It seemed like a genius plan at the time since no one ever came down here, not even the local kids. Plus, months had gone by since the shithole town of Prestonberg and the surrounding area had seen a drop of rain.

It really had been a perfect plan. Hide his supply away somewhere safe and watch as all his competitors got busted and run out of business. With them gone all he had to do was wait a couple of days for the demand to grow and then he could sweep in to corner the market and name his price.

It should have been easy money, but then the rain started. The storm kept dumping on the area, washing out roads and overwhelming what normally were placid creeks and ponds. Right away Scooter realized the trouble he was in. The two forty-gallon drums containing his stash were sitting right in the middle of the system that was about to

Hot Off the Press

be under water as the runoff system did its job. They were right in the path of a shitstorm and so was he. Best case scenario they get battered from the pounding, ruining his hard work. Worse case they break free for the cops to eventually find and trace back to him. As someone with two strikes on his record already, this would mean some serious jail time, and that was something that Scooter wanted no part in. Which is why he found himself out in the middle of this storm, wet and miserable.

Stepping through a circular opening at the end of the tunnel, he finds himself in a large room, about half the size of your average gymnasium. The walls are each covered with dozens of openings of various sizes, some as large as the tunnel Scooter just stepped from, while others are much smaller. The ones on the far wall, what would be the north facing side, is already spitting a steady stream of water into the room. Things are about to get very wet.

In the center of the room is a raised platform, the surface still a good foot above the rising water levels. In the middle of it sits a pair of light blue containers, the drums filled with his future earnings. Smiling, he steps into the room, noticing that the water has risen to his thighs, and wades towards the platform. Reaching it, he plants both hands and hefts himself out of the water and onto dry land.

The grin on his face disappears as he gets a closer look. Half panicked by what he sees, he stumbles towards the stash.

"What the hell?"

The drums had been moved despite being secured to the floor with some very sturdy nylon rope. Not only had that been snapped and the drums moved, but the bottom of each was ripped out,

A Charity Anthology

spilling the precious contents all over the filthy concrete floor.

"What the fuck?!" he yells at the empty room. The brief shout acts as a valve, letting off some pressure before he continues. "This makes no sense. Who would do this?"

Rival dealers would have stolen the barrels rather than just destroy them. And the cops, they would have packed it up as evidence for when they arrested him. No one would just destroy it. Unless there was some do-gooder running around trying to save his customers from their right to get high and his right to make a living. Somehow that idea was the worst.

A loud splash of something heavy hitting water startles him and draws his attention towards the surrounding water. The anger clouds his face again, ready to punish the person that wrecked his plan, or at least anyone that was unlucky enough to run into him today. Standing up, he challenges his yet unseen target.

"Who's there?"

Looking around the room and not seeing anyone he reaches into the waistband of his jeans and pulls out the Glock he has been carrying with him. The cool reassuring plastic grip rests comfortably in his hand. Anger boils up to the surface as he waves it around threateningly.

"I swear to fuck I will shoot a bitch if you messed with my shit!"

His threat is barely audible over the increasing roar of water flowing from the pipes. Spinning slowly, he scans the room for the source of the noise. Not seeing anything, he looks back down at the mess at his feet. All his plans and work ruined by some asshole. Why did this always happen to him? Frustrated, he is about to stomp his foot down like an angry toddler when he hears a loud scraping sound off to his right. Strolling towards the noise and eventually reaching the end of the platform, he looks over the edge into the muddy water. Not seeing anyone, he instinctively extends his right arm with the gun.

Fucker can't stay down forever, he thinks. Someone is going to pay for his misfortune; he at least had that to look forward to. Not seeing anything, he leans forward a bit more, becoming aware of a shadow moving on the bottom. The water seemed deeper on this side.

Suddenly and violently, something breaks the surface and grabs the gun. No, not just the gun, but the hand and arm it is attached to. Pain flows up and down the right side of his body as Scooter is twisted back and forth with great force. Wrenched around, he is finally released and tossed unceremoniously on his ass. Getting his bearings, he sits up only to stare into a pair of dead black eyes.

Survival instincts kicking in, he raises the gun to defend himself, but it isn't there. Looking closer, his eyes bug out as Scooter sees that his arm is gone at the shoulder, leaving just a bloody mess of shredded clothing and skin. He begins to scream as he feels a tight pressure close on his legs and he's dragged towards the water.

Ouija Printer

Killian H. Gore

I probably should have known something was awry when Levi told me he was having trouble with his printer.

We'd met a couple of months ago at a horror convention and I'd been captivated by the solid wood, hand engraved Ouija boards he was hawking on his stall. Annoyingly, I'd already bought too much and was running low on funds but assured him I'd love to own one of them someday. He probably thought I was simply being polite but, sure enough, when my birthday came around, I knew exactly what I wanted.

"I've never heard of him," came Levi's response when I told him I wanted the demon Kergozu painted onto the Ouija board.

"Few people have, but I've got a drawing from a really old book called *The Last Room* by Caleb Baldwin, I'll send you a pic."

I took a photo on my cell phone, carefully levering open the delicate pages to snap a quick, but clear, shot of the malevolent looking creature.

"Wow! What's the story behind *him*?"

"I don't really know much, there's hardly anything written, I just always really liked the image and… the mystery, I guess. So can you do it?"

Of course he could. Levi was a pro at this type of thing.

"What mystery?"

"I can't remember exactly. I think it was related to a haunted hotel room where things go missing."

Hot Off the Press

A week or two passed before an email appeared in my inbox with an attachment showing the finished design.

"That's perfect," I quickly responded, as I gazed upon the exquisitely macabre object.

"I'm going to be sending it today, if I can just get this bloody printer to work, lol."

The bloody printer never did end up working, I gleaned when I received the handwritten addressed package a few days later. The malfunctioning machine left my mind when I opened my birthday gift and breathed in its sweet wooden aroma and gloriously supernatural vista.

Distractedly I picked up my phone and informed Levi of its arrival but got no response. I assumed he was busy working. He always had a hundred projects on the go.

There was little surface space in my home office, only the top of my printer seemed a suitable enough empty spot to place it.

"Is there anybody there?" I jestingly said once it sat upon its new home, erratically gliding the metal ball casters on the planchette over the numbers and letters before...

Did it voluntarily move over to the YES?

I couldn't be sure. My arm felt a little heavier than usual, more like an ache had manifested around my elbow and urged me to stretch it flush. But that's all it felt like. Nothing to freak out about. Besides, my laptop had pinged, heralding the response I'd be anticipating from a hotel in Alaska that wished me to do some work on their website. I forgot all about the *YES* and headed to my seat to hopefully be informed of their interest.

Despite clicking several times on the proprietor's

name, William Elkind, I couldn't get the email to show anything. It appeared that it was blank, which was odd, until I realized that there was an attachment file – a file labelled *Print-off*.

I opened it but, like the email, the PDF file was just a white page.

"What the heck am I printing off, then?" I said to the laptop. More than likely, it was something my laptop was having an issue displaying so I hit the print icon, regardless, and awaited the beeps. But they were not forthcoming.

Looking over at the printer, it was clearly switched on – a small blue light informed me of this. Usually, by now, it would be kicking into action and spewing out some paper, often directly onto the floor if I forgot to fold out the retractable tray

Again, I tried to print, but to no avail.

Surely the Ouija board couldn't be hindering the process? That would be madness. Although, somewhere in the back of mind, the thought of Levi's printing dilemma leaped to the forefront.

"Seriously?" I said, shooting the Ouija board a frustrated frown.

There was only one thing for it – the tried and tested method of switching everything off. That always seemed to work.

And, just like always, it worked this time.

But not quite *just like always*.

Far from it, in fact.

On this occasion the printer made its beeps and started discharging a sheet of paper the moment I *unplugged* it.

Now it wasn't just my arm that felt heavy. Everything felt heavy. A cold and dark heaviness

Hot Off the Press

that discolored the room and my disposition.

Chug, chug, chug, the printer sounded as the paper collected its ink and clawed its way out.

There must have been some electrical charge left in it. Surely that's all it was. Or perhaps it had a backup battery that I wasn't aware of.

Chug, chug, chug.

Further the paper and its message came into view and I almost didn't want to look at whatever had inked itself upon the white void.

The planchette atop the Ouija board jerked with the chug, chug, chugs, but its motions had no concurrence with the machine.

They were spelling something out.

I didn't want to look but was compelled to as I observed the letters K, E, R, G, O, Z, U through the glass lens.

The room became bathed in a hellish red glow, which emanated seemingly from nowhere.

The paper came to rest on the foldout tray.

I could see the words, but they were upside down. It didn't matter. I could clearly read them.

My light-hearted question to the Ouija board had been answered.

I'm here.
He's taken me.
I'm dead.
Destroy the Ouija board!
He's going to…

The ink had run out. It didn't matter.

The demonic creature glaring at me with ferocious red eyes from behind the Ouija board would finish the message.

Sweet Revenge

Tori Danielle Romero

After endless volleyball practices and early mornings, we finally won the championship and went out to celebrate after. I didn't drink but I still partied my ass off and it was well deserved. Waking up past noon on a Saturday had never felt so good.

I went downstairs to get breakfast and ran into my younger sister, Megan.

"Watch out, he's in one of his moods."

"Isn't that every day?"

She laughed and went to her room. When I walked into the kitchen, he was eating some powdered sugar donuts with one hand, a newspaper in the other, and his belly hanging over the table.

"About fucking time you woke up, don't you think?"

The closer I got to him, the more I could smell him. He was repulsive in every aspect. "We won last night; I was out celebrating late."

"You were probably out spreading your legs for all of them pussy ass boys."

"Jealous, Carl?"

He looked me up and down and every part me of me wanted to recoil and hide. "You're just like your mother. Cheap and lazy."

"Fuck—"

Megan pulled me to the side. "It's not worth it, Nicole. I'll make you some breakfast."

"You don't need to do that."

"I want to. You deserve it after you played last night. You're going to get a scholarship after that performance."

Hot Off the Press

He snickered behind me. I could feel my cheeks flush red and I clenched my fists, but I didn't turn around. He would enjoy my reaction too much. Man, I couldn't wait to get a scholarship and move far away from this town, but mostly from Carl.

Just then the doorbell rang. I opened the door and there was an older lady with wild, stringy hair and thick glasses. Beside her was a younger child in a wheelchair holding several boxes of girl scout cookies.

"Hello there. Would you care to buy a box or two of our delicious girl scout cookies?"

"Oh…I…"

"Please, every box we sell gets our name in a big pool of prize money that will help us get young Missy here a new pair of orthopedic shoes and braces. Right, dear? Then maybe she can finally get out of this wheelchair."

The young girl smiled.

"Of course, just one second."

I ran upstairs and went through my pants from last night, pulling out a couple of crinkled twenties before running back downstairs.

"I'll take whatever forty dollars' worth will get me."

The older lady grinned wide; all her teeth were stained black and several of them were missing. The young girl smiled but her eyes told a different story. She seemed sad.

"Bless your heart. This will help us more than you know. Plus, these cookies are to die for!"

I smiled back. "I'm sure they are. Thank you both and have a great day."

Carl was no longer in the kitchen, so I put the boxes on the counter and found my sister cozied up

A Charity Anthology

on the couch with two-fold-up tables set out for us.

"Bon appétit!"

"You're truly the best sister ever."

"I know, right?"

We both laughed.

"You seriously need to stop letting him get under your skin so much, though. I find ignoring him works beautifully."

"It's just the audacity of it all. I don't understand what Mom sees in him. She's beautiful, hardworking, smart, and has settled for some out-of-work, lazy asshole. Make it make sense."

Megan shrugged. "I don't get it either. Let's just hope they don't get married because I will never call him dad."

"Same."

I took another bite of my delicious, scrambled eggs and flipped through the channels but almost every one was showing some big news announcement. I turned up the volume.

Escaped convict, Nadine Prescott, age 65, has kidnapped Tessa Carmichael, age 8, who is in a wheelchair. They have been traveling up the East Coast selling poisonous girl scout cookies. Some may include human feces and various body parts. If you see anyone fitting their description, please call the police immediately. Do not answer your door. Nadine Prescott is to be considered armed and dangerous.

Holy shit. I look over at Megan and just as I'm about to tell her about them coming to the house, a loud bang comes from the kitchen. Megan and I run into the room. Cookies are spilled out everywhere and right next to them is Carl, blood pouring out of his mouth. I reached down to feel his pulse.

Hot Off the Press

Nothing.

"What the fuck? You can't be serious. That's who was at the door? The escaped convict and her kidnapped girl scout?"

"Yeah… they seemed okay. A little off, but… we should call the police!"

I grabbed the phone and Megan put her hand over mine.

"I think we can wait for just a little longer, don't you?"

I thought about it for a moment and then put the phone back down. My heart was racing but all of a sudden a huge weight seemed to lift off my shoulders.

"Plus, what were you thinking paying forty dollars for cookies?"

"Best forty dollars I ever spent."

We both laughed and looked down at Carl's lifeless body.

Mr Taylor

Sarah Schultz

It was a late evening in the prep room of Morgan's Funeral Care, and Jessica decided to wrap up for the night. She rolled her decedent into the back of prep and covered him up with a sheet.

"G'night Mr. Taylor." Jessica always spoke to the decedents as if they were still physically here on Earth. She enjoyed her job. She has been in death care for over four years now, graduating two years ago from Mortuary School. She loved being an embalmer. Seeing how happy the families are when they see their loved ones look like they are still here, just sleeping, is an amazing feeling.

Jessica locks up the funeral home, sets the alarm, and goes home to her cat, Salem. She makes herself a nice pasta dish along with a glass of her favorite red wine and continues watching *Dexter*. Not the New Blood Dexter, the Miami Metro Dexter.

She gets a notification of motion at the funeral home. The establishment is family owned, and the Morgans are out of town this weekend. Jessica and Anna are the only embalmers there. Jessica opens up the camera on her phone as she sips her wine and sees a dark shadowy figure at the end of the hallway across from the prep room.

She texts Anna and asks if she is there. *No*, Anna replied. *I'm at Tom's house. Why, what's up?*

Jessica screenshots what she sees and sends it over. Anna sees nothing. Jessica pulls on sweatpants and a sweatshirt to protect herself from the chilly October weather. *I'll go scope it out. Weird you can't see anything.*

Hot Off the Press

She drives the two blocks down to Morgans'. The building is dark except for the nightlight in the back office that stays on when the building is closed anyway. Jessica gets out of her car and walks to the back of the building where prep is located. She unlocks the door, inputs the code, and slowly walks down the hall turning the lights on.

She hears sounds, like someone working, from inside the cooler area. She grabs her pepper spray and slowly opens the door. The prep room looks as if it had never been closed by her tonight. She looks around, and silence falls. She says hello several times, no reply. She thinks of Mr. Taylor, her decedent from today, and dashes to the back of prep. He was... gone.

She sees blood, purge, and gunk on the floor. She hears the sudden sound of slurping from the cooler. She cautiously ventures to the door and peeks in the little window. There he is, Mr. Taylor, slurping up other bodies and enjoying every last one of them. He turns and sees Jessica. She screams and dashes for the door. He moves quickly for a dead man. He's in front of her, blocking the door.

She makes her way into the office area and hides. She hears him rumbling around, but he doesn't find her. She falls asleep under one of the desks. She wakes to her alarm ringing. She realizes where she is and the events of last night.

Anna sent her three messages asking if she was okay. As Jessica gets up to text her, Anna is already walking in. "Uh, what the hell, man? You are covered in body fluids. What happened?"

Jessica explains everything. Anna looks at their board and asks who Mr. Taylor is. There was never a Mr. Taylor checked in here. Jessica checks the

A Charity Anthology

entire prep room, everything. No sign of him. Anna was right.

Later that day, the medical examiner dropped off a body. "He was called in by Officer Bell. Serial Killer. Vicious. Found in a lake nearby."

Jessica asked his name.

"Mr. Taylor, they called him."

Anna and Jessica's eyes bulged out of their skulls....

My Summer Job

Singh Lall & Maya Lall

All I needed was a bit of cash, just a little to tide me over to the next semester. Every other job was taken, so I signed away two weeks of my summer to a clinical trial. Or so I thought… There were thirteen of us all together. After each being assigned a number I got thirteen, the unluckiest number, at the time I did not realise how unlucky I was. At least number one didn't have to endure the torture of watching what was to come. For he was strapped to a table, the clinician brandishing a rusty saw, his delight unwavering. His intermittent chuckles cutting through the screams of terror as he placed the video tape into the player. *Organ Harvesting for Dummies*.

A Charity Anthology

Blue Light of Death

Justin Terrell

Darkness isn't only what you see when you close your eyes, but also what you see when you close your mind. The light you want so badly to believe to be there isn't there when you're falling deep into a pit of nothingness. Some say the world you create is the world you deserve. Believing in yourself isn't easy, but believing you're a failure sure is. We all want to be perfect, but none of us are. We're all the same with various differences, but deep down we're literally all the same. One thing that connects us is the blue light we all look at.

Think about the guy standing next to you with a suit and tie on the train. On his phone, looking important, like he's making stock trades or something. You're both waiting to get to a destination where you'll walk away and do whatever it is you do. He's no different than you, as you're both on the same source of transit. What makes him better than you? What makes his life more worthy of good fortune than what you have gotten through life? Because he has more money? Because he's dressed well? We all use the bathroom the same way, after all. No one should consider themselves above another, this guy gives everyone smug looks and retracts when someone is near him like he's going to catch the poor man's disease. The difference is... your throat isn't about to get slit, and his is.

As the blood from the rich boy's throat sprays across the wall, the passengers all stare into their phones unaware that a man is dying right by them. I realize by simply holding my phone in one hand and knife in the other, relieving someone of their life, that I am invisible to the bystanders - they're all so oblivious and absorbed in the world of what they call social media.

The actions presented are overlooked by tweetogramers chasing likes, begging for everyone to like and follow, telling a group of people they don't know or care about that it's their birth month and to send wishes. If you're needing to beg the internet for birthday wishes by subtly mentioning it's your birth month, day, hour, I feel like it's time that you no longer have that opportunity in the future. So my gift to you is this switchblade in your jugular. Blood sprays as you gasp but can't move. Good bye and happy birth month.

Standing in this line of people, among other mindless drones, the body drops and it just progresses the line forward. Moans and sighs come from all around for having to step over a speed bump in the line. All of this for a restroom line at an event no one even wants to be at. We're just here because we were told it's cool to attend.

Who even are these musical acts? When did someone with one hit streaming song on soundcloud become the biggest star that no one's ever heard of? Fuck them too! This guy's all-access pass will help with that, so a slight jab to his kidneys and kick in the groin will make it mine since I actually need the access for something important. Yet another body hits the ground and no one sees it happen.

Your favorite artist isn't your favorite artist but this algorithm is generated to make you think you're in love with something that is subpar and lacking

A Charity Anthology

talent. How do you feel now about your favorite artist's tattooed face, Lil' whatever the fuck word he coughed up that morning? Who just invited a guy with an all-access pass to the stage to sing along to a song no one knows the words to. The 150,000-person crowd explodes with cheers and glee, a sea of blue lights visible from the stage with everyone live streaming, not watching anything, but their heart emojis flood the screen as his temples are simultaneously penetrated with spring loaded knives and his neck cut clean with a serrated blade for all to hear the gurgling screams and tearing skin.

The security tries to calm the overzealous cheering crowd, unaware of what is going on just behind them, while others are watching from the stage gawking at the females removing their shirts. Not even noticing what just happened among the sea of blue light screens lighting the way.

This is your world, this is what you've become. Mere drones, slaves to your algorithms. Chasing likes, chasing unearned gratuity and attention. Loving everything you're told to love because it fits the mold of this acceptance-based reality. People fear comets hitting earth, Armageddon and war. This world is already finished, this world has already been destroyed by an algorithm-generating popularity contest.

Darkness isn't in the minds of killers, or the downtrodden and depressed. Darkness is created in the blue light of your screen and the mass herd of hive minded fools. The likes, followers/subscribers, views you amass will never amount to anything or make you a great person. You might make a couple hundred dollars showing your tits while you eat a pop tart, but you're still no different than the rest of us. Your generous bank account doesn't make you better than the person you just laughed at for not having name brand shoes. Your software generated music doesn't make you a better producer of music than the kid sitting in his room picking up a guitar for the first time. Your likes, followers/subscribers do not matter in a world where I can relieve you of your soul in a matter of seconds. It's a cutthroat business we live in, but you'll never see it coming if you're buried in a fantasy land where an AI liked your six-thousandth selfie. That blue light you see is the blue light death of humanity.

A Charity Anthology

Do the Devil's Work

Dean Kilbey

July 2022
The Hope and Anchor pub.

The smell of stale piss hits you before you even open the door. That doesn't stop people going in there though... it's cheap... bloody cheap! Cheap enough to drink away your memories and strong enough to make you forget your troubles.

You can still smell the piss though.

It's fair to say that Jim Peters likes to drink, although it'd be more realistic to say that he's a fucking pisshead. That wasn't alway the case.

London 2012

It's a warm night, the roads clear as thirty-eight-year-old Jim makes his way home from a twelve-hour shift stacking shelves at his local supermarket. His eyes tell you he is tired, but you wouldn't know it. He's screaming out Michael Bublé tunes like he's auditioning for the X-factor.

The screen illuminates as the phone rings. *Unknown caller.* He dismisses it. It's 3am, nobody should be calling him at this hour.

He takes a swig from his water bottle and continues driving.

His phone chimes again. Only this time the screen says *DON'T YOU DARE HANG UP!*

This freaks Jim out and he dismisses the call even quicker this time. He turns the radio off. Even Bublé can't chill him out now. He's anxious. He's

Hot Off the Press

thinking it doesn't make sense.

Who is this person?

He must have imagined it. Yes. It's the only explanation. He's tired – it makes sense. He has been working flat out this week. Those tins of processed peas won't stack themselves.

He rubs his eyes and decides to put the radio back on.

There's no music coming from it, just white noise. He changes the channel. Still nothing... and again... the same thing. He can hear a faint humming.

He turns it up... then nothing. Complete silence.

Suddenly a dark voice comes across the radio. "Hello, Jim. I need you to kill someone for me."

He slams his foot on the brake, his eyes wide open, heart pumping out of his chest. It feels like he is being punched from the inside. The car spins out of control and he smashes into a tree, blacking out.

Three minutes later he opens his eyes. The engine is smoking, blood is dripping down his face. His leg is numb.

Phil Collins is on the radio. *In the Air Tonight* is playing.

Jim leans forward to turn the ignition off. He lets out a painful scream... "Aaggghhhhhh! Fuck!"

He's not a doctor, but seeing his bone hanging out of his thigh like a bloody lamb shank, he knows it's not good.

He reaches for his cell phone and tries to call an ambulance. But before he gets a chance, the phone rings. This time a number shows... 06660 666 0666. He doesn't want to take the call but feels he needs to.

Reluctantly, he presses 'Accept' and listens...

A Charity Anthology

Silence....

Then the same creepy voice speaks.

"Thanks Jim. Now that wasn't so creepy, was it?"

The phone line goes down. He's confused.

Who was it, and why was he thanking me? What the fuck has just happened?

He looks down at his leg. The slice in his thigh is big. It looks like a cheap handbag full of scraps from the butchers.

He glances around. The driver's side door is hanging partially off. He needs to get help. Jim manages to drag himself out and slumps on the leaf covered ground.

He can see a shape under the car. Has he hit something? He drags himself to inspect the lump. As he gets closer, he realizes what it is... "God, no! No, no, no... please nooooooooooo."

The phone dings. It's a message. *Thanks again.*

It was in all the papers.

Missing schoolgirl killed by drunk driver.

Jim Peters, a thirty-eight-year-old divorcee from Romford, Essex, was sentenced to ten years yesterday, for driving under the influence and for the unlawful death of a minor. The kidnapping charges were dropped, being there wasn't sufficient evidence to convict. Mr. Peters pleaded guilty to manslaughter on the grounds of diminished responsibilities, yet he insists he was not drinking at the time of the incident. The victim, Cassie Robinson, aged nine, who up until the accident had been missing for over eight weeks, was last seen attending a sleepover with three other girls from

Hot Off the Press

school. According to friends, she just vanished. Unconfirmed reports suggest they had been playing with a Ouija board, which the parents strongly deny.

10 years later…
August 2022

Jim, now forty-eight (but looking much older than his birth certificate suggested) is back in his regular place.

His haggard, emotionless face, no doubt caused by the regular beatings he received in C block during his stint, stares into the remainder of the flat beer in the bottom of the glass. No one likes a drunk driving schoolgirl killer. You're only one place behind the nonces in the prison league tables.

It's been six weeks since his release.

He's now on benefits. It's not a lot, but it's enough for him… he doesn't eat anyway. Drink however, well that's different. No job, no prospects of getting one, and to be honest, no interest in getting one. He just plods along now, his head filled with the images and screams from that traumatic night.

He can't forget. He tries but he never will. He does occasionally sleep, however. That's where the Hope and Anchor come in (although The Dopey Wanker would be more apt for Jim).

After ten pints of *The Bishop's Helmet,* he's normally on his way home and off to bed. It was a bit different today.

There goes the last drop of pint number nine.

He manages to raise his hand, indicating to the landlord Pete that he's ready for the last pint of the session. It would be easier for him to piss his own pint out and drink it, probably taste no different, and just as warm!

He is given his drink, nods to the barman and takes a sip.

A sweet voice can be heard from behind him.

"Could I have a drink please? My mummy won't get me one."

Jim turns around and freezes on the spot. His jaw drops. Soon after so does his pint, which smashes all over the floor, receiving a rapturous applause from the other local deadbeats.

It's Cassie Robinson, the nine-year-old schoolgirl he killed. She is wearing the school uniform she was found in. Head to toe covered in splashes of blood and dirt plus a light tire mark over her once white ripped shirt. The left side of her face is squashed in. You can see her bare cheek bone and she is missing an eye.

"Oh silly, you dropped your drink..." she says in a sweet and innocent voice. "You're so silly. Was it an accident? Was it?"

Suddenly her voice becomes the demonic voice Jim had heard on the phone ten years ago.

"WAS IT AN ACCIDENT? WELL... WAS IT...? ANSWER ME, YOU PATHETIC CUNT... WAS IT? WAS IT REALLY?"

The laughter grew louder and more terrifying.

"Jim? You okay?" asked Pete, the landlord.

Jim turns around and replies, "It was an accident! It was! I swear!"

Pete tells Jim not to worry about it and to go clean up. Feeling confused Jim shrugs his shoulders. The landlord points to Jim's trousers. Jim had wet himself. Feeling humiliated and embarrassed, he

Hot Off the Press

goes off to the toilet. In the cubical he unties his belt and lets his trousers fall to the floor.

The phone bleeps.

A text message comes through.

It was just an accident.

Jim picks up the phone. Another message.

Hello again, Jim. I need you to kill for me, last one, I promise.

It'd been ten minutes and Jim still hadn't returned to the bar. Pete decides to go look. Maybe Jim had already left and he hadn't noticed.

One cubicle was closed but unlocked. He calls out to Jim. No response. Pete then slowly pushes the door open.

"Oh, for fuck's sake!"

Jim had hung himself with his belt, trousers and pants down to his ankles, revealing his also dead cock.

Pete notices the phone on the floor. He picks it up and looks at the screen. It's a text message from 06660 666 0666. It simply reads…

Thanks again for your help.

A Charity Anthology

The Tapes

Danni Winn

Almost nine months after graduating with a degree in journalism, accompanied by years of diving into the art of video editing, Cera has succumbed to a handful of unpaid internships and is inevitably facing a fuck-ton of student debt.

To help combat the increasing sense of failure she's been experiencing, due to her inability to become gainfully employed in her preferred profession, Cera took on a temporary gig at one of the local news stations. Her task was to tackle the monumental hoard of old videotapes stashed in the corner of their basement and catalogue each tape's footage, forwarding her finds to Gary.

He was a mysterious fella. Cera wasn't quite sure what his role was at the station, but he seemed like a mainstay. When Gary walked into a room, folks would straighten up and conduct themselves differently. Cera has learned to follow suit when it comes to interacting with gruff Gary.

Unfortunately today, there was no avoiding Gary, he was awaiting her outside the elevators.

"Why are you late?" he dryly asked.

"Um... the commute here was a nightmare today because of the weather," Cera quietly responded as she dripped with rain. Gary just simply shook his head and motioned for her to follow him onto the elevator, and they descended several floors below.

"You'll be in a different room this evening, evaluating the tapes in there," he said. The doors opened on a floor she was not familiar with and he briskly walked down a dark hallway that seemed to

Hot Off the Press

go on forever. After passing several doors on each side under the flickering fluorescent lights, they arrived at the end. A sign stated 'Authorized Personnel Only', which required a code for access to be granted. Gary stood in front of Cera as he punched in four digits and opened the heavy door.

Cera coughed when she walked into the larger-than-expected room. It was more of a vault, actually. A vault full of dust and disorganization that immediately queued the OCD within her. In the very corner of the massive room, seemingly swallowed by the endless stacks of boxes and shelves, was a desk with a light, a VCR, and a couple of television monitors. Thunder shook the station and the power went out, momentarily putting the building into a blackout.

Cera swore she sensed someone *very* near to her during the moment of darkness. She could smell something sweet and sickly and she became tense. Before she knew it, the power returned and Gary was on the other side of the room, near the door.

How the hell did he manoeuvre through all this shit in complete darkness? she thought.

"I'll come check on your progress in a few hours," Gary said flatly. And just like that, the heavy door slammed behind him and Cera was left alone.

It was now nearly midnight. Several hours had passed with a tower of VHS tapes gone through and Cera was beginning to feel restless in the basement bunker. She got up to stretch and walk around. Strolling through the room, traversing the aisles made up of boxes and filing cabinets, she came across a container unlike any of the others. Worn, yet carefully tucked up on a shelf, with no other boxes sitting close, this one piqued her interest. Upon closer inspection, Cera could see it was tightly tied with twine. She returned to the dimly lit desk, carefully opened the fascinating box, and immediately laughed out loud as she retrieved yet more VHS tapes.

"Not sure what I expected," Cera joked with herself. She plopped down in the chair and spun it around wildly, enjoying the momentary relief from boredom and fatigue. But as the cheap ride ended, Cera's gaze fixated on the box and her curiosity grew.

The tape she put in was confusing for her to decipher. It was not news footage or an interview or anything like what she has been documenting the last few weeks and it quickly made her feel uneasy. It seemed to be of a person filming themselves walking down an unlit hallway, quietly humming. Muffled screams could be heard as a door slowly opened to reveal a haunting, candlelit scene. Cera's eyes widened in horror as she watched a truly sinister spectacle.

A young man in only his boxers is seen shackled to the floor and he is absolutely terrified. Surrounding him in a circle are several men in suits with black hoods concealing their identities and applauding the entrance of the humming man. The camera now slowly scans the nefarious gathering and their growing excitement as the captive becomes more frantic.

"Vote now," ordered an unseen voice. The circle of hooded men began to throw up different colored cards from their pockets, casting uncertain ballots.

"Black seems to be the winning card," said the unseen voice. Applause erupted from the faceless, suited men with the camera cutting to close-ups of clapping hands. Time seemed to stand still as Cera tried to process the violence unfolding before her eyes, fighting back bile rising from her stomach. In a fury, the young man's screams of fear were silenced with a swift series of powerful punches to the head and stomach. He lay there defenseless, dazed, and bloodied. A black gloved hand reached into frame to grab the victim by the hair, forcing him to kneel. The camera is now stationary as the humming man drags something along the concrete, something sharp. Silence befalls the group of spectators as they part to allow a cloaked man to enter the circle and approach the victim, giant fucking sword in hand. He raises his arms high and quickly slashes down, beheading the young man. Blood gushes from the severed arteries and the head rolls out of frame.

Cera gasped so loudly she didn't hear anyone enter the room. "I see you found your next assignment," said Gary.

A Charity Anthology

Open Doorways

Peter F Mahoney

Einstein hinted at it; not in so many words but he did raise the idea of matter and energy being a continuum- and a change in energy changing the state of matter from solid to liquid to gas and vice versa. What he *hinted* at was aberrant energy breaking down the barriers *between* places, between states of existence.

This happens in war. I've seen it. I'm not talking simply about the material destruction and waste that inevitably occurs with our single most stupid act as a species but about the *consequences* of all this uncontrolled energy being released.

After an explosion, if you know how to look, you can see what is best described as a 'shimmering', of reality getting a bit thin. Frequently you can't see this because of all the dust and shit flying around (And realistically, in many situations you want to be hugging the ground to avoid said shit) but sometimes you can- and very rarely you can see things moving in it.

My first time was in the Balkans in the 1990s. There had been some of the usual unpleasantness moving through villages where neighbours had ruthlessly killed each other. Sad shapes lay as still silhouettes in burned out houses. Clouds of flies would rise up from them as we moved carefully past (carefully in case said neighbours had left trip wires or other booby traps for unwary multinational troops; no one is neutral, right?).

Anyway, one of the UN brethren was less alert

Hot Off the Press

than he should have been and caught a wire. There was an insignificant click and a 'ping' as the device armed. Then an evil sharp crack, a flash of light and a dreadful rattling as ball bearings sprayed out and struck building walls. Mr UN was shredded; lucky for me as he took the bulk of the metal cloud. I was sprayed by torn fragments of man, uniform and webbing and my hearing disappeared. I think I was concussed; I next remember lying on my back looking up at the bright blue sky and marvelling at the clouds. Then I remembered what had happened and very carefully turned over onto my front. There was a slippery clear liquid seeping into the floor which stained my already ruined clothing. As I turned, I looked straight into the eyes of one of them.

I think, at first, he was as surprised as me. Our ruined room (of stone) now blended with his (some sort of wooden structure). The join between the two looked insubstantial and bubbled; that's the best description I can give. I'll call him a Demon until I learn of a better term. The Demon looked a lot like an elf from the *Lord of the Rings* film series. He was naked but had crossed his legs modestly. Bizarrely he was eating from a silver boil-in-the-bag ration pack. Next to him on a wooden kitchen table lay a badly decomposed body. The features were swollen, the belly bloated. Liquid fat ran out of the corpse; now I knew the source of the clear liquid. The heat generated by the body was obscene. The Demon was casually using this to warm up more of his rations. Two further silver packs lay on the corpse's torso. Using a spoon, he delicately finished his first portion, carefully folded the empty silver

A Charity Anthology

bag and placed it under his chair then opened another. The smell of decay was physical. I was pushed beyond nausea. Not him though; no- nothing seemed to bother him. The second pack was opened and sampled with obvious satisfaction.

The whole event must have only lasted seconds, maybe thirty, maybe less. I know what you are thinking- shock, concussion, and the product of a stressed imagination. That's what I hoped. The scene shimmered and I was left with the more routine horror of a brutalised building and a vapourised colleague. And damaged hearing.

Thing is, it happened again. The next explosion was during a tour in Iraq. Nothing as close this time; just a whistle, a 'whump' and a building shaking. Air was pushed out then pulled back; all very standard. What wasn't standard came next. The shimmering. The blending of two environments and the alien room. This time it was different. No corpse on a table and the Demon was wearing clothes. Not his relaxation time I thought. The room had more depth. At the far end were sheets of semi-transparent plastic. In the darkness behind this, figures moved. They were indistinct – a combination of the poor light and the plastic sheets but there was a wrongness about them. They hinted at terrible injury but if that was right how could they still be moving? I can't explain how the room from the Former Yugoslavia now linked with a space in Iraq. Maybe I was the link? Maybe once you've had one of these experiences a terrible connection is formed? The Demon did seem more substantial this time and I wondered if he was going to try and walk over. And bring his friends with him?

Hot Off the Press

You might be dismissing this as PTSD- after all, isn't that something so many of us are said to be suffering from? Thing is, I wonder about this and have a theory that it's all a bit more *Jacob's Ladder* and less routine mental health. Watch the film; you'll see.

I'll know soon. It is happening again. There are no shortage of explosions here in Afghanistan and I think that has made the barrier even thinner. Question is, if they arrive again will they come across here – or should I try and go there? Can't be much worse than here, can it?

Knickers

Tony Sands

Polly peered into the drawer and frowned.

"Ya see what I mean?" said Gemma.

"Yeah, yeah," replied Polly without turning her head. "What is it?"

"A hole. In the drawer."

"I know it's a hole, it's obvious it's a hole. But, what I'm asking is, what's the significance of this particular hole? What makes this hole more special than any hole that has come before it?" Polly sniffed as if she had just laid down a winning argument in a very important court case.

"That hole," stated Gemma, in her deadliest, most serious tone, "is a black hole."

Polly stood up straight, looking at her neighbour and wondering if she had been drinking. "A black hole in your knicker drawer?"

Gemma nodded. Polly inspected beneath the drawer, but she could see no sign of any kind of hole. Just the wooden panel bottom. Polly looked inside the drawer again, puzzled. The hole was still there, black and ominous.

"It's only inside it. I think that's how black holes work," Gemma said.

"What do you know about back holes?" Polly asked.

"Not much, only what Darren told me. He seemed to know quite a bit, said he saw a movie. He said it was alright but could have been better. Can't remember what he said it was called, I think it had robots in it though, the film, not the title… maybe the title… hmm."

Hot Off the Press

"And Darren is?"

"My boyfriend... well, I guess, ex-boyfriend now that I think about it," Gemma mused.

"What?"

"He got a bit too close to the hole," Gemma said sadly. "It pulled him in. Disappeared right into it. I tried texting him to see if he was alive, but the messages didn't go through. When I called it went straight to voicemail. I don't think there's service down there... in there... down in there."

"You're saying your boyfriend fell through that hole?" Polly sneered cynically.

"Yup. I mean, he was more kind of pulled in, rather than fell in. I tried to grab him, but I had a cup of tea in my hand and couldn't find anywhere to put it down in time. It's such a shame, he was going to take me to an Italian restaurant that night, I love Italian."

"And when did that happen?" Polly was getting bored of this charade now.

"Last Tuesday."

"Have you reported it to the police?"

"No, I don't think the police know much about black hole abductions. Do they?"

"I wouldn't know," sighed Polly. "I'm going to go home now and watch some telly, or maybe stare at a wall, I don't know yet. Anything but stand here and listen to this utter nonsense."

"It's not nonsense," Gemma muttered defensively. "It's real, all of it. I promise."

"Really?" laughed Polly sarcastically and plunged her hand into the hole.

"No, don't, that's what Darren..."

But, before Gemma could finish her sentence Polly was pulled into the hole in one sudden

A Charity Anthology

movement. Gemma managed to grab her left foot, but was left holding a pink slip on shoe as Polly's legs, then feet, disappeared into the blackness, wriggling madly. Polly didn't even have time to scream. Gemma pondered the shoe, then dropped it into the hole after its owner. She looked down, without getting too close, then shut the drawer and sat on the bed.

"Oh, bother," mumbled Gemma, crinkling her brow with a deep frown. She was going to have to find somewhere else to keep her knickers, that drawer just wasn't suitable anymore

The Room at the End

Patrick Krause

The bedroom, once a dusty relic to a long dead woman, was now a sterile, spartan space with no furnishing aside from a bed, toilet, and a television on the wall. The room was transformed into a quarantine space for sick family members, a legal requirement after a new disease quickly wiped out 60% of the world's population. Eric, the room's newest inhabitant, thought of it as a shrine to disease, fear, and decay. The smell of disinfectant invaded his nostrils. This room, like the house, once belonged to his mother and had known only sickness, insanity, and death.

Eric sighed and sat on the edge of the bed, looking to the floor. There, faded but visible in the wood, was the final evidence his mother had lived there. In her last years, Alma had begun using a spirit board to speak with her dead sister. Every night, from outside her door, Eric could hear Alma whispering and the scrape of the planchette across the board. When it had become an obsession, the board was taken from her. In her desperation and insanity, Alma used her fingernails to carve a rudimentary board into the floor. After her death, Eric had tried sanding and painting over the etching, but its wretched design refused to be erased.

Eric swung his legs up onto the bed, turned off the overhead light, and quickly fell asleep. The room inhaled deeply, as if waiting for something within the encroaching darkness as the soft light from the bulb faded out. Eric did not dream that first night nor did he hear the scratching from within the closet.

The first week of isolation passed without incident. Each morning Eric woke to the sound of latches turning on a slot in the door, and his breakfast tray pushed inside. Grumbling, Eric turned on the light and began his day. After breakfast, Eric would turn on the television to watch the news and pass the time. Temperature checks were done daily, confirming the fever was not relinquishing its hold.

On the seventh night Eric's sleep became restless. Laying on his stomach, his left arm fell over the side of the bed, fingers just out of reach of the spirit board carved into the floor. His arm moved like a heavy pendulum, finger pointing down toward the letters, spelling out a word: A-Z-A- when Eric's eyes shot open with a blood-curdling scream as he broke into a cold sweat. Trembling, he pulled himself into a fetal position. From the dark of the closet, a throbbing pale green light pulsed. Before passing out, he heard the whisper of an ancient name, "Azathoth," followed by a woman chuckling before everything went black.

The same visions haunted Eric the next evening, and on the ninth night Eric awoke suddenly, throwing himself against the door and walls, covering them in blood from his pounding fists, screaming, "Azathoth is here! She brought it here!" His pajamas lay in tatters on the floor. Eric begged anyone who could hear him for help. But the only one listening was the darkness inside the closet.

Eric sat in the far corner weeping, opposite the closet he now stared at. The faint sound of discordant flutes and the maddening beat of drums filled the room. He placed his hands over his ears to

Hot Off the Press

no avail, and no scream could escape his ever-widening mouth. Inside the closet appeared a pile of bones and crushed skulls covered in excrement, piss, and cum. Sitting upon this throne of abomination was a woman in a long, hooded robe of crimson.

She looked up, the hood opening to reveal the face of his mother, Alma. Her visage flickered back and forth from the young beautiful woman she once was to the weathered, old crone she had become before she died. The flesh appeared to be bleached a pure white but hung so loosely off her skeleton, the skin gave the appearance of melting wax. Her eyes were the deepest black, and within that black the stars of the cosmos. A mucous covered tentacle pushed its way out from the hairless mound between her legs, causing the robe to fall open revealing her nude body. It slowly probed the air and stroked Alma's thighs. A deep, open wound on Alma's left thigh was visible, bright with blood and pulsating muscle, and as Eric stared at this horrific vision he was fed images of his mother's last days. Alma was using the spirit board, calling out to her dead sister but her plea was answered by something not human, something older. Then, Alma using her fingernails to carve the board into the floor and ripping the skin from her thigh to create a planchette. The final grotesque image of Alma greedily chewing off her pinkie to use the bone in the eye of the planchette seared into Eric's mind. Tears fell from his eyes, but the encroaching madness and complete terror kept his screams silent.

Tentacles pushed their way out of Alma's eyes, nostrils, and rectum. Dripping with a primordial slime, they slithered down her body and across the floor. Eric could not avoid the groping touch of the sickening proboscis, nor avoid watching as Alma's body split from her anus to the space between her bulbous breasts. A cavity opened revealing a gaping maw of nothingness and everything the cosmos had ever vomited out. The drum beat intensified and the house shook with the booming cry of "AZATHOTH!" from deep within Alma. The tentacles wrapped around Eric's body and pulled him toward the thing that was once his mother. Her lips broke into a parody of a smile as she welcomed Eric back into her womb. She spread her legs as wide as possible, arms outstretched, and in the cracked voice of a decrepit crone, said "Come to me, Azathoth."

The tentacles withdrew into Alma, her skin knitted closed over her reclaimed son. Sighing with pleasure she caressed her bulging stomach, cooing, promising to bring Eric to the altar of his new god, Azathoth. The last tentacle pulled back into Alma's mouth; the tip caressed her red, cracked lips. The hideous tongue like appendage made a slurping sound as it licked the drool that dripped from the corner of Alma's mouth, and finally withdrew into it. Eric's face was pressed against Alma's skin from inside her body, mouth open in an unheard scream. The room exhaled, and the horror in the closet faded into the nothingness from which it had come.

The house sits as empty and silent as a charnel house, avoided by passers-by who gossip about what had happened inside and put off by a growing, fetid odor around the property. So it waited, this empty house with a reputation for darkness, longing for new flesh to inhabit it.

Blue Moon Bottling

Monster Smith

Insects danced feverishly under the soft glare of the streetlight as the shiny white milk truck inched its way down Arcane Boulevard like some sort of preordained harbinger of death. Flames lapped at the sky and fires raged out of control while mysterious creatures of the night ripped and tore through the town, turning the place into a scene straight out of a Lucio Argento flick. Meg ducked her head and the kids followed suit, hoping to go unnoticed as they made their terrifying escape.

Things were bad and Paul couldn't believe his eyes. He'd never seen anything like this before. Things had gotten completely out of hand and there was nothing anyone could do about it, save for martial law. Everywhere they looked people were mutating and turning into unrecognizable globs of flesh, hair, and blood, and he steadied the wheel as they slunk past the old movie theater, or what was still left of it.

People were infected and rapidly changing, all thanks to the Blue Moon Bottling Company. The dairy distributor was Arcane's one and only supplier of milk, and it was known that anyone who'd drank their product within the last seven days needed to be quarantined immediately, no questions asked. Failure to do so could result in serious and severe consequences, from which death was more than likely imminent.

As they slowly crept along the blacktop, a man began to cry out in horror as a large pulsating blue ball crawled up his forearm, eating straight through his flesh to the bone. It was like someone had poured acid on him, disintegrating his arm like a vat of cotton candy. The thing continued its merciless ascent up the poor sap's neck, pausing directly on his face before engulfing the rest of his skull.

Another victim was covered from head to toe in what appeared to be hundreds of tiny blue boils, each one throbbing and phosphorescent under the dull white glow of the large looming headlights. It was hard to watch, but at the same time, he couldn't look away. Suzy was afraid to peek, but Marko tried his best to get a glimpse of what was out there, his father angrily scolding him to get back down before something bad happened to them.

"You better get your ass back down in that seat boy, or you're going to get us all killed," snapped his father, his eyes unflinchingly facing forward so as not to draw any unwanted attention from the mutant marauders.

"I'm sorry, I'm sorry. I just want to see," said the boy, more frightened now of his dad than he was of the creatures lurking outside the borrowed milk truck.

"It's alright honey, your father's not mad at you. Just stay in your seat until we hit the highway, then you can look all you want, okay?" said Meg, her heart racing like the wind.

Mad at both of his parents for lashing out at him, he began to sulk and pout, unaware of what was really taking place just outside the walls of the vehicle. He was too young to understand why his father was dressed in a milkman's uniform and why they'd stolen the truck and were trying to leave the area. Had he known what was truly out there, he

Hot Off the Press

wouldn't have disobeyed the strict instructions and put their lives at risk.

"What is that...?" he managed to get out before erupting in a fit of hysteria, coming to the realization that what he was seeing was in fact a real-life monster of some sort.

Immediately Meg grabbed the boy and cupped her hand over his mouth, stifling the ear-piercing scream that was about to be unleashed. However, despite her best efforts, the monstrous crowd had caught wind of the commotion and decided to in turn attack the truck, accosting the occupants like they owed them money. It was a full-on assault, and Paul shuddered at the sight as they converged on their newly acquired target.

Suddenly, an enormous eight-foot-tall creature with two heads – one human, the other a large blue lump with a set of what could only be described as eyes – cleared a path as it made a beeline straight for them. It had a long slimy arm-like tentacle protruding out of its shoulder, and it let out a bone-rattling roar as it smashed against the hard metal exterior, denting the truck's frame. Suzy screamed, feeding every nightcrawler within earshot with the tears from her sweet fear-filled cries.

Out of nowhere, three similar-looking blobs of goo with legs began to mount and trounce the vehicle, giving it a thorough thrashing right alongside their giant two headed compadre. Marko nearly wet himself as they were besieged by what he said were the *scary monsters from his nightmares*, and although it sounded absolutely insane, his father knew exactly what he meant by it. There wasn't a word in the English dictionary that

A Charity Anthology

could explain what they were witnessing, it was utterly life changing.

Afraid for their lives, Paul slammed on the gas, and the truck shot out of there like a rocket, flying down the road at speed, tires smoking in the rear view. Meg held onto both children as tight as she could, making sure they didn't somehow vanish in the mad dash. And that's when something tickled the underside of her bicep, causing her to instantly flinch and jump back in her seat.

Peeling herself away like she was going to catch the flu, she looked down at her little girl in awe. Suzy's skin was crawling with thousands of slimy blue insects, causing the poor girl to panic and scream for her momma. Apparently, earlier in the day, she'd been so thirsty that she couldn't help herself and she'd downed a nice tall glass of ice-cold milk without anyone knowing, since it was the only thing around to drink at the time.

"Oh my god! Paul," screamed Meg, as her daughter began to shake violently, her head separating and splitting in two, revealing a nasty worm-like creature inside the gushing, gaping hole where her face just was.

A Better Place

Hal C. F. Astell

It was five hours into her shift when Melody Johnson realised that she was dead.

It was a hard realisation but an unavoidable one. After all, the story that had arrived on her desk at the time-honoured Federated News Agency was about her. Only tangentially, but about her, nonetheless. She validated it.

That was her job, at a company with a motto of "all the truth and nothing but the truth". She and they prided themselves on never sending a false story on to the press. They even joked about it, often suggesting that their terminals simply wouldn't allow it.

The newsworthy story was about someone else.

Brent Clay, two-term Republican senator for the state of Alabama, skipped lanes and crashed his car into oncoming traffic. He had a fundamentalist Christian track record of speaking up for traditional family values and voting against LGBTQ+ rights. He was found unconscious in the wreckage with his trousers around his ankles and the severed penis of a fifteen-year-old Filipino boy in his mouth.

The boy's younger brother was in the back seat; the politician's wife of three decades and their five children were not. Senator Clay is in critical condition at St. Andrew's Hospital and the younger boy is being treated for concussion. The passenger was declared dead at the scene from massive blood loss.

What Melody couldn't unsee was the car that Clay had crashed into. It was a baby blue Fiat

A Charity Anthology

Bambino. *Her* baby blue Fiat Bambino. She could tell, not only because it had been her baby for seven years but because the photos accompanying the wire showed her slumped over the steering wheel, surrounded by blood.

She was dead. But she was at work. She couldn't deny that. She even pinched herself to be sure. It was the same grey-walled cubicle in the same green-themed office. It was the same streaky carpet under her feet, the same comfortable chair under her butt that she'd fought hard to procure and the same terminal under her fingers that she'd worked at for seventeen years. Clearly she was at work. And she was dead. All the truth and nothing but the truth, right?

So what was going on?

Was she in the Twilight Zone? It felt like it. She racked her brain but couldn't remember actually getting to the office. She'd been drinking coffee for hours but her mug was still full and hot. And she hadn't had to visit the little girl's room once. Maybe she *was* in the Twilight Zone. What would that mean?

Did she have to atone for something? She couldn't think of anything. She hadn't led a perfect life but it had been a worthwhile one. She'd married a good man, Derek, who had passed a couple of years earlier from a resurgence of cancer. They had twenty-two good years and no bad ones. Two children, Ethan and Rachel, both doing well as they moved on to their own lives. Ethan and his wife Sarah had blessed them with a grandchild, who was cute as a button and would be two years old in August.

No, she didn't need to atone. She couldn't think

Hot Off the Press

of anything important left undone or unsaid. Derek had gone before her. The kids knew that she loved them. Chloe would when she grew old enough to understand. Ethan would see to that. Why hadn't she just moved on to be with Derek?

But maybe this wasn't about her. Maybe this was about her job. She told the truth for a living and she'd died as an afterthought in someone else's news story. Had she been given a karmic opportunity?

"Donald Trump, the twice impeached former president," she wrote, "was convicted today on eight counts of fraud, wire fraud and conspiracy to commit fraud in conjunction with his attempts to subvert the 2020 election. The judge is scheduled to pass sentence on Thursday morning."

She re-read what she'd written with her proofreader's brain and clicked to submit. Nothing happened. Maybe this wasn't it either.

Or maybe she'd gone too far. After all, Trump couldn't be convicted today if he hadn't even been tried, right? That couldn't be true and the FNA terminals wouldn't allow anything that was untrue.

She deleted her final sentence, changed "convicted" to "charged", proofed again and clicked to submit. This time it went through. The terminal accepted it as truth and that meant that it must be true. She'd died a day early. She wished she could have been alive to read that in the newspaper over breakfast.

For the next hour, she submitted stories that, in her opinion, needed to happen and should have done long ago. The terminal didn't take them all, but it accepted plenty of baby steps. Russia and Ukraine will meet in Ankara to talk peace. A bipartisan bill

A Charity Anthology

to bring single-payer healthcare to the United States passed its first hurdle. George R. R. Martin submitted a first draft of *The Winds of Winter* to his publisher.

Gradually Melody realised that she was fading. Her fingers hit the keys but the keys didn't depress. Maybe it was time. She'd fixed enough. She felt a mild stab of annoyance that she hadn't had Fox greenlight a second season of *Firefly*, but she wished it away. Some things need to be let go.

One thing wouldn't. She pulled up the story of her death, summoned all the energy she could and added, "Mrs. Johnson left the world a better place." Submit. Accepted.

She faded. She smiled. Dr. Ngor at her bedside at St. Andrew's Hospital watched electronic blips flatline.

"Mr. Johnson," he told Ethan, who was holding his mother's hand, "she's gone. But it looks like she was ready."

Misphonia

Alain Elliott

He'd had this all his life. Most people found it amusing when he told them, let out a short giggle before realising he wasn't happy about it. Eating meals was often excruciating because of it. Often, he had to hold back his instinct to scream at the noise. Those noises. And now he was in the middle of a meal that he could barely afford, slowly getting more annoyed. Well not that slowly actually, he was quickly fuming inside.

The guy on the table behind him was chomping down on his food so loudly that he couldn't believe that no-one else seemed to notice. Joe was sure he was doing it specifically to annoy him personally. This guy had his back to Joe, so he couldn't tell what he was eating but he could tell that he was eating open-mouthed. Big open mouthfuls, one after the other, chewing down with his teeth each time. That's why the sound was literally painful to him. Every slurp, gulp and scoff as he devoured his meal. It produced a fuzzy feeling around his ears that wasn't pleasant in the slightest. He could feel it around his head and on his hair, it made him scratch at his ears. He couldn't take it anymore.

"Are you serious?" Joe had turned around, but the guy still didn't realise he was talking to him and just continued munching away. Joe scratched the side of his head again, in a vain attempt at distracting him from both the noise and his tingling ears.

It wasn't working though. He put his head down, now facing the table and placed his hands on the

A Charity Anthology

back of his head trying to think of anything except where he was right now. It had gone too far though; nothing was going to stop him.

Joe wrapped his fingers around the fork that was alongside his plate. He took one long deep breath in and stood up. In one quick motion he turned and with his right hand stabbed the guy in the head with the fork. He still had hold of the fork as it stuck in the man's temple, and he held it there as the guy screamed and everyone in the restaurant looked in their direction. Before anyone else could react to what was happening, using the fork, Joe pulled the guy down backwards still in his chair until he hit the floor. He then pulled the fork out, blood speckles spraying through the air on to Joe's white shirt and the white tablecloths. He then thrust the fork back down into the open mouth, stabbing the tongue hard. He could feel the fork put three holes all the way through the tongue and with that he dragged the fork out while splitting the tongue into four bloody slithers that now looked like they were moving independently until they fell back into the man's mouth covered in blood and saliva.

For a couple of seconds, all Joe could hear was the guy choking on his own blood but then he heard more screams. Everyone else in the restaurant could see what had happened and Joe was aware of all the people around him. He was knelt next to the, now silent, guy but all Joe noticed was the noise he couldn't hear. No chewing, no chomping, no slurping, no nibbling, no crunching, no biting, no scoffing, no nothing. No-one was eating.

Hot Off the Press

The Mysterious Case of the Patch of Damp

Tony Mardon

On arrival home, Johnson headed for the stairs, eager to see his wife of many wonder filled years. Throwing open the bedroom door, he was greeted not by his wife but by a patch of stagnant, odious damp, situated just below waist height on HER side of the bed.

As he approached the bed with a sniff in mind, Johnson's wife emerged from the en-suite, red in face, clearly fatigued and as naked as a marrow. Johnson assumed the worst; a supernatural Patch of Damp had somehow gotten to his wife and was attempting pure evil upon her very being. He thought quickly...

"Darling, take my side of the bed away from the devil's oil slick. I shall sleep by your side upon the floor ready to fight for your very soul if needed!"

Justina did as instructed and, still visibly exasperated, climbed into the unblemished section of the marital love restplace.

As Johnson settled upon the harsh but cleansing stone floor, he noticed, at eye level, a 'glistening' a metre or so away. His heart sank for he knew what it meant. He clawed forward, spasming as his theory proved correct. In his hand he held tight Justina's panties... the patch of damp inside had caught the light. It shimmered, just as the larger stain had. A second Patch of Damp! She had been entered!

"She is already taken," he declared, sobbing. "Satan's Big One has invaded her very essence via her tasty and meaty love hole. The evidence is clear."

A Charity Anthology

Stunned, he stood and approached his wife's extremely old-fashioned dressing table and reached for Justina's equally old-fashioned sharp pointed, silver-plated hair brush... He plunged the end down... down... down... again... again... again... into his wife.

"I have destroyed the patch of damp that has claimed my dearest Justina!" he declared triumphant. A larger, redder, slightly stickier Patch of Damp oozed out now from HIS side of the marital sex stronghold.

"Irony!" he considered. "I have created a Third Patch of Damp in the cleansing of my beloved Justina, who was also a cleaner and could have been leaner."

Could have called her Gina.

Here endeth our story but, unknown to Johnson, he had unwittingly created Patches of Damp Four and Five as Justina had also pissed and shit herself moments before death...

Being Normal

Astrid Addams

The man slunk into the takeaway, his favourite cheap fried chicken place. The cheapest place he knew that was 'Living Only', even in the kitchen. The man ordered his usual and manoeuvred his huge backside into a plastic chair facing the door. He checked his phone for the thousandth time, nothing new from the woman. She had messaged eleven minutes ago to say she had dropped her kid off and was on her way. The man was nervous, she would be the fourth woman he had met since the advert. Two had been hard charmless bitches with ugly, rude brats. One had even been *dead!* Not what he was after at all. Even worse, they had all looked at him like he was the freak! The man was used to that, but things would be different from now on.

His usual arrived just as the woman did. Alive, but she wouldn't look him in the eye as they awkwardly shook hands. She was thin, her hair tied up in a bun, slap on her face, she wore trousers and a blouse as if she were attending a job interview. The man asked what she would have to drink and bought her a coke and offered her a piece of fried chicken. The woman shook her head and thanked him for the coke with a small smile. She was taller than him, hell her five-year-old probably would be too. The man started to eat his fried chicken and chips with extra salt.

"Can you cook?" the man asked through a mouth full of chicken.

"Yes." The woman had a quiet voice, her cheeks flushed.

A Charity Anthology

"What's your kid like?"

"Tilly? She's no trouble," the woman mumbled.

"Do you have a pic?"

She fished out an ancient iPhone with a cracked screen and held it out to him. A living girl with Rapunzel hair grinned up at him in a way that made him want to smile. She might do, if she could be trusted to keep her mouth shut. The man licked the salt from his fingers.

The woman took her phone back, biting her bottom lip.

"When are they kicking you out?"

"Two days' time." He heard the strain in the woman's voice and smiled, she was desperate enough for anything. He paused, looking at her over his chicken bones as she squirmed before him.

"You happy with what we discussed?" the man asked eventually. The woman nodded. "And you and the girl will be able to stick to the rules?" Another nod, the woman looked like she was about to cry.

"Alright, bring your kid to meet me at the park across the road when you pick her up." The man tried to keep his voice monotone. "If she's a good girl, you can move in rent free."

Two days later, the man helped the woman and her daughter move into his mother's house. The neighbours watched from behind twitching curtains and tittering hedges. They all knew he was a loser; his mother had told them so. How he was too stupid, disgusting and worthless to ever get married and probably too impotent to give her a cute grandkid. Now she was dead he could prove them all wrong with his slim wife and their pretty little

Hot Off the Press

girl. The man waved smugly at them, introduced the woman as his wife at every opportunity, the woman smiling politely back at them. The little girl clutched her baby doll and kept quiet, as the old bitches cooed over her and he boasted.

Once the show was over, the man ushered his new family into the house and locked the door. The woman cooked dinner and they ate together. Then she did all the drudgery his mother had forced on him without complaint until eight, when as agreed, the woman and girl said goodnight and went upstairs. The man locked the door after them and went back to the front room his mother had died in and switched off the telly. Lastly, the man opened the basement door and headed down to his dark lair, where his mother had kicked him all those years ago.

The darkness was comforting, it contained his true self and his own stuff. The man snatched up the part melted Zombie Santa Claus: Axe Murderer Edition he'd found in a skip as a boy whilst hiding from his mother after Christmas and held it to his chest. The bastard never came for him, but at least he'd got the toy.

He selected his favourite illegal, uncensored film. The familiar black and white of the best *Human Centipede* film lit up the darkness. He smiled as he watched the man and his mother, so like him and his own. Now he'd smothered her, his mother's corpse sat beside him on the plastic covered sofa, arms and feet in specialist chains, her rotten teeth snapping behind her Undead Deluxe Muzzle.

The man was free at last, especially now that he had found the perfect cover family to make him look like everyone else. He was at liberty to build his own Human-Undead Centipede hybrid and finally enjoy the 'Age of the Living Dead', which made the possibilities for the man's creative mutations endless. The man patted his mother's shit-covered night dress and smiled. His mother snarled at him, as if she still had a pulse, as the hero on screen began to work with his staple gun. The man reached into his pants.

Mirror Mirror

Chris McAuley

I hear knocking in the dead of night.
It's not coming from my house door.
It's coming from inside my bedchamber.

In the year of 1736, I sold my soul to the Devil. I don't mean that in haughty metaphorical terms. I wanted to recapture the love of my youth and I wanted revenge on the wrongs which were cast upon it.

It all began with a desperation for money, I wanted to buy a plantation. A private place which would provide me with some income as I pursued a desperate and forbidden love affair.

David had been a slave of my father's. He was tall and handsome in a gangly sort of way; he had a way of seeming proud even when he dared not raise his eyes to those who deemed themselves his masters. I was enchanted by his dark wavy hair, so unlike the fair haired and skinned men who carried the whips and ran my father's farm.

Frequently I would find myself following David, pretending to be picking flowers for a bouquet at the side of the road. At times, I would stand and watch him as he built stacks of hay in the barn, allowing him to see me loosen my hair so that it flowed down onto my purple dress.

Eventually we became lovers and I knew that I had to free him and to do that, we need anonymity and money. With money, we could flee and he could pretend to be my hired hand for an estate as we whiled our days and nights together against satin sheets.

A Charity Anthology

I concocted a way to steal some of father's money but I was discovered. He found out my design and had David flogged while I watched. His beautiful dark skin was turned slowly into a flowing crimson as the lashes continued. My father then turned his attentions to me and I felt pain which was unimaginable, I only endured a quarter of what my love had been forced to until I passed out.

I did not say that my father was a good man.

I felt as if I had been cursed by God and like another with a similar fate, he who was cast from the sight of the creator to fall to Earth. I felt rage and a desire for revenge. Feeling a kinship with the fallen angel, I turned my attentions to the wise women of the villages, enquiring about the forbidden dark magics. Powers that would return my David back to me and rid the world of men like my father.

Eventually I came upon an old Jew, a man who had reportedly wandered the world and who served the dark lord himself. He gave me a mirror by which to cast my intention upon. It was called El Draco – the Dragon's Mirror. It had lain in service to a powerful European nobleman who had used it to entrap his enemy's soul.

That night I lit the candles on my bedroom floor, their shimmering, dancing light illuminating the occult symbols scratched with my bloody fingernails across the room. Small, intricate marks full of magical meaning and personal power. I swept the canvas from the heavy frame of the mirror, the engraved, grotesque faces projected from the wood leered at me as I breathed my intention on the thick glass.

My efforts, had, at that moment seemed to come

Hot Off the Press

to naught. Feeling again cheated and betrayed, I collapsed, naked onto my bed, allowing my thoughts to be carried into the warm dark of nightly oblivion.

Until I was awoken by the knocking.

I looked first towards the window, for surely this sound was more of a tapping. A tapping on glass.

I then moved my head slowly and with dread towards the mirror, illuminated by the last, flickering flames of the candlelight.

I caught sight of a dark and bloody hand knocking at the glass.

David's tortured and still bloody face, half eaten by the crows that had pecked at his unburied body turned to me. His left eye had turned into a milky, yellow boil of pus.

With his bloodied fingers and with his final tortured moments still immortalized on his torn flesh, he wrote the word...

Why?

A Charity Anthology

The Wolf in the Darkness

Craig David Dowsett

David was a banker from the city. He had just moved to a quiet rural location with beautiful scenery filled with a dense woodland. It was calm, peaceful and away from the noise and buzz of the big city. His house was located at the end of a long lane which was surrounded by forest either side. He had a fair daily walk to and from the train station through the forest which he usually enjoyed. That was until one evening on his walk home, night drawing in, David started to sense something or someone watching him in the deep darkness of the forest.

Still a fair way from the safety of his house, his senses started to heighten. David was beginning to feel uneasy, when suddenly something dashed across the lane far in front of him. It was big, dark, and vanished so quickly. Feeling spooked, David picked up his pace. His briefcase was the only thing he had with him, and all he wanted to do was to get home fast!

He kept looking left and right almost in a panic, then out of nowhere a huge wolf like creature appeared directly in front of him. Its fur was jet black, its dark red eyes fixed directly on David. He could see its breath in the cool evening air. David froze as fear set in. The creature charged at him, snarling and drooling, teeth as sharp as daggers pierced David's skin ripping the flesh from bone again and again. All David could do was try to crawl away as the evil creature was just too powerful to fight off.

Hot Off the Press

Blood was everywhere by now and as the creature came to deliver the final bite, it paused. As if toying with David, it held his arm in its mouth and was just looming over him, its big dark red eyes staring straight into David's! It then let out an almighty howl which sent shivers down the spine of David's body as he knew the end was near.

Slowly out of the forest more creatures appeared, black fur, big sharp teeth, mouths drooling, savouring the meal to come. They charged towards him, ripping his body limb from limb, tearing his face off. David was paralysed, helpless as the creatures were eating him alive. By the end of it nothing was left of him, not even bones. All that remained was a briefcase that to this day still lays in the deep darkness of the forest waiting to be found...

Waiting with the wolf in the darkness...

The Rise of the Sanguinista

Cortney Palm

The rain beat down with an aura of hatred onto the large, marble steps of the cathedral. Anez' frail frame undetectable between a giant white column and the ornately carved mahogany door. She didn't bother to look up at the angels smiling down upon her, she wasn't worthy of their grace. Silent tears fell, mixing with blood and rain cascading away as if they never existed.

Lightning cracked, illuminating The Square, not a soul in sight. Who would blame them? The tenacious wind and rain created an inhospitable center full of mud, erasing all the footprints of the lively day. It was dark out. No one went out at night in this city. Fears came out to play in the darkness. A resounding thunder shook her soul.

"Oh God!" Anez cried out, "Please forgive me!" She slammed her fist upon the door making no sound. A whisper of wind tickled her cheek and fear, or was it shame, drew her body into a tighter ball.

Silent in the wind, Jecken descended and perched upon the gargoyle statue taking no heed to the rain that slammed against his pale skin. He cast his senses out towards the square, finding a mouse trapped in a tragic dance between eternal damnation and new life. If you could call it life. He watched the angels open their wings, no light shouldered out. He scryed further and noted a foul scent.

Jecken hissed. *Not tonight, you don't, she is mine.* "To what God do you refer, child?" A voice rang in perfect pitch regardless of the storm. Anez looked up at the dark figure. He was tall and thin, wearing a cassock. She noticed the look he gave her, as impassive as it was and quickly wiped the blood away from her mouth. "It's okay, it'll be our little secret, let's get you dry, shall we, do come in."

He reached an impossibly pale hand out towards her. She considered reaching out for it, clinging on to some form of support or love offered from anyone who would give it, even if it was a stranger. He was a man of God, therefore he could be trusted, right?

Lightning flashed and the man's true face was briefly illuminated revealing the sickly nature of the tainted beast beneath the hood. Anez screamed, but the creature grabbed a hold of her and dragged her inside.

Just before he could pull the doors shut a guttural, bone-chilling sound erupted right outside. Anez was thrown to the ground. Quickly gathering her bearings, she scooted her body towards a wall. A look of horror befell her face as two creatures engaged in a tangled battle of fangs and blade.

Without hesitation, Jecken had leapt off his perch and flung open the giant door with little effort. His strength incomparable to man. The foul entity dropped the child. Jecken howled and tore into the tainted holy place, spinning in the air and landing with agility and grace, then equally as quickly drew out a silver blade. The entity he faced simply stood, discarding his cassock to reveal his grotesque form.

"Bravo, bravo. Brilliant display of brute strength and tenacity Jecken. But I am afraid, you're rather too late. The poor little street rat already sold her soul to me." The demon opened his palms as if in complete surrender. "Don't you see? I have won."

A Charity Anthology

"You disgust me," Jecken spat, "you have no power of your own, you are weak, without human souls you are nothing." With a flash of silver Jecken drew his blade upward, slicing the demon's face. The mark sizzled where silver met flesh and foul blood boiled on the mosaic tiled floor, the beast roaring in agony and anger.

Jecken heard the girl whimper as well. He turned to her and noticed she was changing. The demon leapt to the ceiling, clinging to a painted cloud. Jecken spun in a circle, by the time he looked up, the foul beast was descending upon him! Without delay Jecken knelt down and came face to face with arch-angel Michael, Jecken's eyes wide.

Knowing what to do, he twisted his blade in hand and pointed it upward. Instantly hot blood showered around him, covering the mosaic depiction of the high angels. A resounding cry erupted from the corner. Jecken shoved off the demon and pulled out his sword, racing to the little girl. He was too late. She was floating in the air, her eyes rolled back, dripping blood, her body distorted. Laughter echoed through the cathedral.

Jecken whipped around towards the demon. "Let her go!"

"She sold her soul. Even God can't save her now." The sickening laughter continued. Jecken screamed and charged towards the demon, cutting off his head with one swift motion and landing with ease, bowing down, uttering some last rites for the tainted soul.

He turned to see the little girl's body distorted and broken. Jecken pushed off the floor effortlessly and ascended into the air; he held the body of the girl and lowered her back to the cold floor. "You are forgiven my child, you are loved, you are worthy of grace."

Jecken revealed fangs, and bit into his own flesh, his wrist pooling with blood. "You can join the holy fight with me, your soul will be free, but you must drink." He allowed his blood to drip into her mouth.

Anez began to feel her body again as a light entered her heart. She tasted the sweet iron and craved its sustenance. She opened her eyes and looked up into the stranger's face, undeniably handsome gray eyes staring into hers.

She had one question for the one who came to save her. "Who are you?" she managed to mutter.

"I am a demon-slayer and the Knight of Christ." Anez knew what that meant, she may have freed her soul from one set of chains but bound herself to yet another.

She nodded, amplified strength returning to her. "Teach me."

A Long Way Down

Bill Oberst Jr.

Before a coffin shop in Tlalpujahua on the main street down the hill from the church above the bodies below (the ones from the accident you know) last night I laid me down or was laid down more naked than not in a dew-damp dark to the barking of some stray Sirius off towards the stone steps of the monument.

Mightily pissed I mightily pissed and splashed wavy glass with American crass looking in at those sad wood boxes (much better ones back home I think I thought) and, eyes closed, stretched me out in the doorway of the coffin shop in Tlalpujahua.

Cold.

Would grow colder.

Didn't you notice the light burning, Señor?

Inside Voice a.k.a. Research

Adam Marcus

Everyone's a screenwriter. It's the only area of artistic expression that EVERYONE thinks they can do. Because as long as you have a pencil, paper, iPhone or computer, have a rudimentary education (second grade will do) and have SEEN a movie, ANYONE can write one! For fuck's sake, I had brain surgery in my early thirties and my brain surgeon pitched me a script during a follow-up visit! The left side of my face was so palsied, I looked like I had had a stroke, but that didn't stop Doctor Brainenstein from pitching me his medical thriller. My dental hygienist was literally scraping my teeth when she tried to sell me on her boyfriend's movie idea... not a script, just a fucking idea! I never ask for help at the grocery store for fear that the kid sprinkling water on the vegetables thinks he should have a three-picture deal at Netflix!

Oh Jesus, baby, what is that? Duran Duran? She knows I'm working. I hate that. And when did she start liking the eighties. That's my jam. She knows I'm trying to concentrate and write and what... they're having a dance party? Okay, whatever man, just ignore it...

Where was I? Oh yeah...

And what nobody really gets is that the rare moments when words magically flow from your fingertips, come from thousands of hours of words not flowing. Of shitty ideas. Of imbecilic notes from imbecilic people who have the money to produce what you write, so they get to say what stays and what goes. And for some reason it's always the good stuff that goes. ALWAYS! And no one is an expert, anymore. I mean, I got pigeonholed into the horror box when I was in my early twenties. I've spent more time coming up with ways to murder teenagers than any prolific serial killer. More importantly, I've spent more time learning how to get an audience to care about those teenagers so that when they're slashed or chainsawed the audience gives a shit! And none of it seems to matter. Nope! Now anyone can slum in the horror genre. When I started, we were thought of as no better than pornographers. Now, we're the only ones who are guaranteed to make money. So everyone wants in. All you do is comedy? Well, whatever, have a trilogy of horror sequels! Heck, take two! But worse of all nobody respects…

Research! Countless hours of research, and no I don't mean watching other people's movies or just stealing an entire plot from a Hong Kong film and calling it your own! No, real research about real things. Real things that move you to want to write stories that can change the world. Well, it's time this pigeonholed bird spreads his damn wings. Time I write something that matters. And even though no one will ever know that I've spent hundreds of hours spelunking into the darkest parts of the internet… And they won't understand the psychic scars of looking at the most evil, vile shit these White Nationalist fucksticks do during their free time… It's time I stand up and take a stand and say something that matters!

The hideousness that's out there. The way these people think and feel… my God! And the things they do to perceived enemies. I mean, you can't

Hot Off the Press

believe what's gone on out there. There's this one woman, a reporter, who infiltrated one of these lunatic fringe sites and these racist maniacs came in the middle of the night and they murdered her whole family. The whole God damn family. Husband, her kids... even the family cat. Tore them to fucking pieces and all while she was in her office writing. She was there! The whole time. These sick fucks came in and taped everyone's mouths shut, started playing some Barney the Dinosaur Kid Club songs... you know to cover the noise... Then... you wouldn't believe this... they slowly sawed her kids heads off with a rusty handsaw while she was just typing away... or worse yet, doing research on the same pieces of shit that were murdering her family. And they took their time. I mean, the husband was forced to watch his kids get decapitated. Fuck. But I think the worst part of all of it, is that they left her alive to find them all... I mean, she has nothing. Totally stripped her of her world, her life, her loves. All because she threatened to expose a tiny corner of their sick, filthy, backwards-ass world. These mutherfuckers who always think might is right. WTF?

Damn it. Why is that music so loud? What are they doing down there, moving furniture? Wow Hon, you know I'm trying to work... Whatever, I'm gonna ignore it. I will not be pulled from my path. I'm finally going to make a difference. Make a stand and expose the real horrors in the world... I'm just gonna ignore it.

Man, it's noisy down there. Well, I'm not going down there and getting distracted. I gotta get some writing done tonight. Or maybe some more research...

A Charity Anthology

The Circle Inside the Triangle

Jonathan Patrick Hughes

November 9th 1984, 6:22 pm.

It's a cold and brisk evening as William Laughner gets ready for his date with his dream girl while blasting Mr. Roboto through his speakers. His mother abruptly comes into his room with a smile from ear to ear. William, who is wearing nothing but a towel, is highly embarrassed.

"Mom! Don't you know how to knock?"

"Oh, calm down, son. You act like I haven't seen it all before." William rolls his eyes as she approaches him. "You're turning into such a handsome man, and I am so very proud of you, William."

"Thanks Mom, but I am trying to get ready for a date with the woman of my dreams. Do you think that we could have this sentimental moment another time?"

Mrs. Laughner smiles and responds, "You are just like your father." She gives him a hug, fixes his hair, and then exits the room closing the door behind her. As William finishes getting dressed, he glances at a polaroid picture of Sherri Streno, a beautiful blonde cheerleader who has a smile that could light up Las Vegas. The picture alone puts a smile on William's face. You can see that he has deep feelings for her.

William looks out his bedroom window and sees a 1978 LTD Ford station wagon slowing down in front of his house. Full of excitement, William states, "She's here." He quickly rips off his towel,

Hot Off the Press

gets dressed, brushes his teeth, swishes around mouthwash just in case he gets to lock lips with his date, and then races down the stairs while screaming in delight, "Mom, Dad, I'll be home around eleven."

William's parents meet him at the door and tell their son to have a good time. His father, William Laughner Snr, reaches into his back pocket, pulls out a rolled up twenty-dollar bill, and puts it into his son's hand. "Have a great night, son."

"Thanks Dad. Don't be surprised if I end up staying with this one for the rest of my life."

"Don't rush it, you're young and have your whole life ahead of you."

William smiles, grabs his football jacket off the coat hanger, and heads out. As William approaches the vehicle, his parents take a sneak peak out the window to get a glance at the woman their son is going out with.

Mr. Laughner wraps his arm around his wife's shoulder and whispers into her ear. "Do you remember our first date?" She looks at him and smiles as he kisses her forehead.

The vehicle takes off into the night. "I'm sorry if I kept you waiting. I just wanted to look extra nice tonight."

Sherri snickers at William, "Is wearing your football jacket what you call… extra nice?"

They both laugh. As they continue driving, Sherri mentions about going to a new Italian restaurant in the neighborhood for dinner and possibly stopping for ice cream afterwards. By the look on William's face, you can see that he has something else in mind. He reaches into his jacket pocket and pulls out two passes to a horror movie

A Charity Anthology

premier.

Sherri, who is not a fan of horror, agrees to go as she can see how excited William is. Upon driving, they get into some traffic. William notices ahead that there is a bridge and they can take the exit right after. Sherri turns on her blinker and moves over on the right, entering the bridge which is also packed bumper to bumper.

William becomes a bit antsy knowing that the movie starts in roughly twenty minutes. Sherri, who hates being in traffic remains calm, and continues small talk to pass the time. Suddenly, a huge gust of wind plows right into the vehicle, causing the car to shake rapidly, with heavy fog in the air. Neither of them can see a thing.

Sherri continues driving inch by inch. The fog clears in seconds, however the vehicle starts making noises as if it's breaking down. Sherri panics while attempting to get over to the far right. Once all the way over, the car gives out. She tries to start it again and again, but the car appears to be dead.

William tells her to pop the hood so he can take a look, and once he gets out of the car, he notices that there is not a single vehicle on the road. Everyone just sort of vanished. He notices lights up ahead which are signals to the theatre for the premier. William talks Sherri into leaving the car behind and that he will pay for a tow truck once the movie is over. Sherri hesitates, but agrees, because she doesn't want to ruin the date. William takes Sherri by the hand and they walk towards the flashing lights.

Upon approaching the theatre, the two realize that there is not a single car in the parking lot. Sherri says, "Where is everybody? I thought this

Hot Off the Press

was supposed to be a premier?"

"It is, I guess not a lot of people know about it."

"If you ask me, Bill, looks like no one knows about it."

They come to the front doors of the theatre and enter into the lobby. They notice an employee at the concession stand and walk towards him.

"Busy night?" William jokes, but the employee just stares at him. "Can we get a large popcorn, no butter, and a large Coke with two straws?" The employee slowly gets their order as William reaches in his back pocket and pulls out the twenty-dollar bill his father gave him earlier. He pays the employee, grabs his change, and they begin walking towards the ticket taker.

The ticket taker, however, looks identical to the guy at the concession stand. William gives him the two passes, he takes them, puts them inside the ticket box and points to the doors where the movie is playing.

As William and Sherri walk towards the theatre, the ticket taker mumbles, "See you soon."

William looks back at him. "What did you just say?" Sherri doesn't want any trouble so she grabs William by the hand and proceeds to walk towards the theatre as the ticket taker stares at them cold and blank.

Sherri and William grab two seats in the middle of an empty theatre as the lights dim and the opening logos appear on the silver screen. The movie ends ninety-two minutes later and they get up from their seats and exit the theatre.

As they leave, the ticket taker is still staring as if he never stopped looking in their direction the entire time they were in there. He watches them both with a sinister grin as they pass him on their way out. While exiting the lobby, William notices two people coming in, looking just like him and Sherri, same clothes and all. They walk past him and Sherri without looking at them, as if they weren't even there.

William, bewildered, continues to watch as the two grab a large popcorn and large Coke, the same order him and Sherri got. They continue walking out the front doors and now Sherri notices two more people crossing the empty parking lot and heading inside, looking and dressed the exact same way.

William tells Sherri to wait while he goes back into the theatre. She doesn't want to wait outside alone in the dark, so she decides to go in with him. They pass the creepy ticket taker on their way back in and once again he mumbles, "See you soon."

As Sherri and William walk inside the theatre, they notice that the seats are full from top to bottom and they are all duplicates of him and Sherri. They both look at each other as the horror increases upon their face. In this moment William realized that he was going to be with the woman of his dreams for the rest of his nightmarish life.

The Present

Philip Rogers

Even though he had spent half the night staring at the ceiling in excitement, Alex didn't need his phone alarm clock to wake him up this morning. As he turned to the red numbers of his alarm clock, illuminating in the darkness as they flashed 6:17, he knew it was finally Christmas morning.

Despite still being half asleep, Alex leapt out of bed, unaware of the crisp cold air of the morning as his feet came crashing firmly to the floor with a thud. Alex bounded forward with an energy and excitement which rarely occurred on a weekday, and despite almost losing his balance in the process he continued to gather speed.

As he made his way down the stairs, he began to regret the various trips to the kitchen throughout the night, but he told himself that would have to wait as he continued stepping down with excitement.

As he opened the door to the living room, Alex's eyes lit up like the tinsel and flashing lights which over accessorized the loaded Christmas tree, a tree that had looked so ordinary when they first selected it. And now it looked even more magical as it lorded over a landfill of presents which had been placed beneath it.

Alex congratulated himself for having the will power not to avoid sneaking a peek earlier and allowed himself a small squeal of excitement as he looked down at all the presents. There were many to choose from, but his eyes were constantly drawn back to a large red box which had been tied up with a golden ribbon. He wasn't sure why it intrigued

A Charity Anthology

him so much, it wasn't the biggest and certainly not the most colourful, but something was calling him to it. He couldn't say why but there was something special about it and he needed to open that one first.

Kneeling in front of the tree, he picked up the red box and began to shake it, even though he knew it wouldn't make guessing what was inside any easier. He placed it gently down on the floor and began slowly untangling the ribbon, but he startled when the voice of his mum behind him broke his concentration.

"That's a very special one for my baby boy," she said softly. Alex winced at the term 'baby boy', which he thought at thirteen he had outgrown, but turned around to gesture a smile before relaying his attention back to the present.

The voice of his father followed cheerfully, "Go ahead and open it son, Merry Christmas." Any caution to opening the present had now passed. Without the need for further prompting, Alex carelessly pulled apart the ribbon and began to rip through the paper, which he had previously found so eye catching. When the paper was removed, Alex lifted the lid of the box to reveal the severed head of his teacher, Mrs. White.

Alex dropped the lid to the floor and turned to face his parents. Alex's mum smiled and opened her arms towards Alex. "No one gives our special baby a C- grade. Merry Christmas son."

Alex's eyes began to swell, and he ran over to his parents to give them a hug. "I love it, can we eat her with Christmas dinner?"

His dad smiled. "It's Christmas son, you can eat anyone you want."

Unsolved: True Crime Hits Home.

Debbie Rochon

The year was 1978. This was the epoch of serial violence. It's as though the payment for the perverse and loose 60s was due upon receipt and there was a precipitous retribution that hung in the air like the aroma that dawns from the flats during low tide. It was the perfect storm of very limited forensic science and no communication between law enforcement agencies. You could literally throw a rock in any direction, and you'd hit a serial killer. Society and damaged DNA crossbred and succeeded in birthing a generation overstocked with bogeymen.

During that year I was a homeless teen in the west end of Vancouver. Some would find it hard to envision, as today the area stands as one of the most expensive places to live in all of Canada. That wasn't the case in '78. It was before Hollywood moved in, before Expo '86 had shown the world what a pretty city looked like and a myriad of the spectators never left, and, it was before the area's self-righteous citizens got all up in arms and took to the streets to push out all the homeless kids and other disposable, underground tragic figures. There was plenty of scum too. Where there is yet to be corrupted innocence, and lots of gullibility, that's where you'll find the darkest, most rancorous users of people; primed and practiced in the art of soul destroying.

So, it was during this highly invisible and anonymous time that I suffered one of the worst attacks of my life.

A Charity Anthology

Winter arrived like an unyielding bully claiming the hallways in school. It didn't feel like there was anywhere you could go to get warm but I was determined to find someone I knew who might know of a couch to crash on so I could get the chill out of my bones. I had a lead on a place, but that had just fallen through. Apparently, this splashy apartment dweller only accepted homeless teen boys and was not interested in a female couch crasher. I was now headed towards Denman Street where a lot of the kids would go and hang in front of places like Hamburger Mary's, looking for a lonely person to buy them a meal. I was bound to know someone there.

My hands were so cold I could barely feel them, but my determination to warm up made the slicing wind tolerable. I would count a lot for distraction. Ten more blocks and I'll be there… I would think of a song I like to distract myself. The Clash's version of Police and Thieves was a solid mantra. *From genesis to revelation, the next generation will be, hear me.* Seven more blocks… pulling my coat closed, sans buttons, to keep the frigid blast of air from dropping my core temperature any further. Six more blocks…

I suddenly felt my feet leave the ground for a second. I was down on my side and was being pulled by a savage force into an underground parking lot. I didn't have time to comprehend what was happening. Before I could get any balance, I was flung down the cement entrance and rolled to a stop. I started to intentionally roll to make some space from this psycho so I could flee. Before there was time to think, move, breathe, the first hit came down. It was so sudden I didn't even know what

Hot Off the Press

happened. Something had hit my head. Without any thinking involved, my hands immediately covered my skull. Bam! Another hit came. Instinctually I threw my bag as far as I could sling it, assuming I was being robbed. But the hits still came anyway. It might have been two more, or maybe three. I couldn't tell you for certain. I was stunned by the smashing.

It had immediately occurred to me, even in that horrible moment, this person was bashing my skull in with a tire iron for what seemed long after I had thrown my belongings to stop it. That's not a robbery. I knew in that second, he was there to do very serious damage, that was his objective. I saw his face. It was white, slender and he had short black hair. After he grabbed my bag, he ran out towards his small blue vehicle. He made off with a five-dollar bill for his efforts.

I got myself up and managed to walk to the entrance of the underground parking lot. I saw a white car driving up and flagged it to a crawl. When it was pulling up in front of me, I fell onto the hood of the car and blacked out.

I must have been out for a few minutes; the next thing I remember is arriving at the hospital where the good Samaritan dropped me. I was seen immediately by a doctor who wasted no time in examining and sewing up my head. He purposely kept me talking during the procedure.

When you have things done to your head and brain area you typically don't get any painkillers because they must monitor your speech and ability to function. I remember he asked me how it happened. I knew I couldn't tell him because there was no doubt a police BOLO with my name on it

A Charity Anthology

circulating out there, seeing I was a reported runaway by the foster care system.

So, I said the only thing that came to mind. The excuse you heard on TV shows and in movies - and everyone knows it's not true. "I fell down some stairs". I was savvy enough to know that neither one of us bought the delivery and he would be calling the police soon. The minute he was finished with the sew job and left the room to get something, I jumped up and bolted out the door.

To this day I don't know how I was able to do that. I guess fear is a mother of a beast. I was able to vanish from the physician's table, but I spent the next month sleeping on a very kind person's couch. A boyfriend of a guy I knew from around, a doorman at a gay nightclub, I think. I literally couldn't stand up for a month without fainting because I had lost so much blood that night. What damage did a half dozen blows to the head with a tire iron do to me? Medically I don't know. Mentally it crippled me real good.

That's why I like horror movies, books, art etc. It's the only genre that acknowledges evil. True evil is out there. I have to assume this guy went on to commit murder. I was the final girl in my own story that night.

The Checklist

Matt Doyle

Item 1: Contact

Even as weak as I feel right now, the phone line is the easiest thing to take care of. One small snip and it's done, ya know? I used to keep spare cables around the place, but I hate mess and seeing broken stuff, so I had to stop doing that. It'd be, like, five minutes and I'd just *have* to fix it and start all over again.

I can't just leave it either, I've *gotta* cut them. I mean, I need the phone and all, but it's landed me in so much shit with the police. Like, last month, I forgot to cut the cables, and when everything kicked off, I panicked and dialled without thinking. I just couldn't stop screaming. They came running, sirens wailing, waking everybody up... they got here expecting a murder scene and found me huddled naked in the corner instead. No intruders, just me, apologising, over and over. In the end they told me not to call like that again or they'd arrest me for wasting police time.

The neighbours stopped talking to me after that.

I just stubbed my last cigarette out on my arm. I think I'm getting too used to it though, because it doesn't really bother me anymore. I stopped cutting for the same reason; I was having to go deeper and deeper to make myself cry out. Back when it still hurt, I could get *really* loud. It took a long time to get used to the idea that people here actually pay attention to me screaming.

Or they used to.

They're good people. I *hate* disturbing them so much. So, no cutting. A couple of packs of cigarettes, a couple of glasses of Jack, fill the bath with ice cubes. That, I can do. I can keep things down to a raspy cough that way. No more voice, no more problem for the lovely people down the hall, and no more awkward conversations.

Item 2: Escape

The flat's quite barren these days. I guess it's more of a room. A studio they call them, right? I used it fill it up with shit. A bed, TV, curtains; simple stuff like that. Now though, all I've really got is two piles of clothes: clean and dirty. Oh, and the telephone, but that doesn't really count on a Saturday.

I kinda like this though. Five years back I had all the stuff a kid could want but it didn't mean much in the end. Getting shot of it all is the only bit of defiance that I can manage. It helps me ignore Saturday until it arrives.

Light bulbs were the most important things to get rid of. After a while I'd start staring off into them of an evening and drift into pretending I didn't feel anything again. *Back then*, they were a comfort. It helped having that big white light I could run down.

I don't need that escape now.

I'm alone.

Having the windows done was a fantastic idea, though. One night, I threw something through them and tried to crawl out. That was a lot of fucking blood. It hurt too, but different than I expected. Even if I still had stuff to throw, I'd never manage to break them now. The joy of double glazing, eh? But

Hot Off the Press

hey, even if I did manage to break them, there'd still be the shiny new metal bars, so it's all good.

Item 3: Entrance

The door's a piece of piss. Simply unlock and leave open, nothing fancy there.

Item 4: Defence

Another good reason to rid myself of stuff. No stuff, nothing to defend myself with. That helps create the right mood. Cigarette boxes, ice bag, a lighter, and a pair of scissors. All bought Saturday morning. All in the communal bins by Saturday evening. The phone is still there but only because I figured it'd be cheaper to buy new cables than a new handset or mobile. Plus, it's so lightweight, I probably couldn't kill a fly with it.

My clothes are fairly raggedy. No metal attachments like zips or buttons. They all fit well too. I don't need belts that way. I used one back then. Wrapped it around my little fist and everything. All that got me was a black eye with my *rent payment*.

A weekly rent payment.

That's what my uncle called it.

Of course, I know *now* that you pay the rent with money. That's why I have a job, right? To pay the bills? Well, that and for takeout Sunday to Friday. No food on a Saturday though. The weaker I feel, the better.

Item 5: Repetition

A Charity Anthology

Hello night. I won't stay long. If you need me, I'll be right here, shivering in my corner, waiting for the floor to creak. Then I won't be here anymore. Not entirely.

I know it's not him.

It's been two years and he either ain't found me or doesn't give a shit. He'll be here soon anyway though, and it'll be real until morning. Five years of Saturdays and he hasn't changed his pattern. He'll just stroll on in reeking of booze, jeans around his ankles.

It's fucked up. I do this because I know I *don't* need to be afraid anymore.

Every week I give the world the chance to mess with me. To step right on in and do something.

Anything.

Hurt me.

Please?

There's nothing there to stop it but it doesn't happen. I *need* something to happen. I feel like shit. My gut is ripping its way out of my body trying to get away, but there's nothing to get away from, so I make myself live through it all again just to make it make sense.

Five years of not feeling right if I even *think* of feeling right.

That's why this checklist exists.

Creak.

Also from Red Cape Publishing

Anthologies:

Elements of Horror Book One: Earth
Elements of Horror Book Two: Air
Elements of Horror Book Three: Fire
Elements of Horror Book Four: Water
A is for Aliens: A-Z of Horror Book One
B is for Beasts: A-Z of Horror Book Two
C is for Cannibals: A-Z of Horror Book Three
D is for Demons: A-Z of Horror Book Four
E is for Exorcism: A-Z of Horror Book Five
F is for Fear: A-Z of Horror Book Six
G is for Genies: A-Z of Horror Book Seven
H is for Hell: A-Z of Horror Book Eight
I is for Internet: A-Z of Horror Book Nine
J is for Jack-o'-Lantern: A-Z of Horror Book Ten
K is for Kidnap: A-Z of Horror Book Eleven
L is for Lycans: A-Z of Horror Book Twelve
M is for Medical: A-Z of Horror Book Thirteen
N is for Nautical: A-Z of Horror Book Fourteen
It Came from the Darkness: A Charity Anthology
Out of the Shadows: A Charity Anthology
Hot Off the Press: A Charity Anthology
Castle Heights: 18 Storeys, 18 Stories
Sweet Little Chittering
Unceremonious
The Nookienomicon

A Charity Anthology

Short Story Collections:

*Embrace the Darkness by P.J. Blakey-Novis
Tunnels by P.J. Blakey-Novis
The Artist by P.J. Blakey-Novis
Karma by P.J. Blakey-Novis
The Place Between Worlds by P.J. Blakey-Novis
Home by P.J. Blakey-Novis
Short Horror Stories by P.J. Blakey-Novis
Short Horror Stories Vol.2 by P.J. Blakey-Novis
Keep It Inside & Other Weird Tales by Mark Anthony Smith
Everything's Annoying by J.C. Michael
Six! By Mark Cassell
Monsters in the Dark by Donovan 'Monster' Smith
Barriers by David F. Gray
Love & Other Dead Things by Astrid Addams
Bone Carver by Gemma Paul
Shadows of Death by Dee Caples*

Novelettes:

The Ivory Tower by Antoinette Corvo

Novellas:

*Four by P.J. Blakey-Novis
Dirges in the Dark by Antoinette Corvo
The Cat That Caught the Canary by Antoinette Corvo
Bow-Legged Buccaneers from Outer Space by David Owain Hughes
Spiffing by Tim Mendees
Go It Alone by Monster Smith*

Hot Off the Press

Novels:

*Madman Across the Water by Caroline Angel
The Curse Awakens by Caroline Angel
Less by Caroline Angel
Where Shadows Move by Caroline Angel
Origin of Evil by Caroline Angel
Origin of Evil: Beginnings by Caroline Angel
The Vegas Rift by David F. Gray
The Broken Doll by P.J. Blakey-Novis
The Broken Doll: Shattered Pieces by P.J. Blakey-Novis
South by Southwest Wales by David Owain Hughes
Any Which Way but South Wales by David Owain Hughes
Appletown by Antoinette Corvo
Nails by K.J. Sargeant*

Art Books:

*Demons Never Die by David Paul Harris & P.J. Blakey-Novis
Six Days of Violence by P.J Blakey-Novis & David Paul Harris*

A Charity Anthology

Follow Red Cape Publishing

www.redcapepublishing.com
www.facebook.com/redcapepublishing
www.twitter.com/redcapepublish
www.instagram.com/redcapepublishing
www.pinterest.co.uk/redcapepublishing
www.patreon.com/redcapepublishing
www.ko-fi.com/redcape
www.buymeacoffee.com/redcape

Printed in Great Britain
by Amazon